TEEN ~~~

...ngs I'm seeing without you.

PRICE: $20.00 (3798/tfarp)

THINGS I'M SEEING WITHOUT YOU

PETER BOGNANNI

DIAL BOOKS

DIAL BOOKS

An imprint of Penguin Random House LLC

375 Hudson Street, New York, NY 10014

Library of Congress Cataloging-in-Publication Data

Names: Bognanni, Peter, author.

Title: Things I'm seeing without you / Peter Bognanni.

Other titles: Things I am seeing without you

Description: New York, NY : Dial Books, [2017] | Summary: "When tragedy strikes, Tess drops out of school and moves in with her funeral director dad, forcing her to examine life, death, and the boy she thought she knew and loved in a brand-new light"— Provided by publisher.

Identifiers: LCCN 2016037372 | ISBN 9780735228047 (harcover) | Subjects: | CYAC: Grief—Fiction. | Fathers and daughters—Fiction. | Funeral rites and ceremonies—Fiction. | Dropouts—Fiction. | Classification: LCC PZ7.1.B6448 Thi 2017 | DDC [Fic]—dc23 LC record available at https://lccn.loc.gov/2016037372

Printed in the United States of America

1 3 5 7 9 10 8 6 4 2

Text set in Minion Pro

For Kathy Bognanni

1

The morning after I dropped out of high school, I woke up before dawn in my father's empty house thinking about the slow death of the universe. It smelled like Old Spice and middle-aged sadness in the guest room, and this was probably at least part of the reason for my thoughts of total cosmic annihilation. The other part I blame on physics. The class I mean. Not the branch of science. It was one of the last subjects I tried to study before I made the decision to liberate myself from Quaker school, driving five hours through Iowa farm country to make my daring escape.

I did the drive without stopping, listening to religious radio fade in and out of classic rock, which sounded something like this: "*Our* God is an awesome Godddddd and . . . Ooooh that smell. Can't you smell that smell? The smell of death surrounds you!" All I could smell was fertilizer. And as the empty fields and pinwheeling wind turbines passed by my window, I tried not to think too hard about how I had let things get to this point. And I tried even harder not to think of the improbable person I had come to love, who would no longer be in my life.

But back to the universe for a moment.

There seems to be no real consensus about how it's all going to end, and that's what had me worried in the predawn hours. If the worst is going to happen, as it always does, I'd at least like to know some details. But current theories are too varied to be of any real help.

Some people think the Big Bang is just going to happen in reverse. Like: *BANG!* Everything to nothing! Deal with it fools! Other people think that outer space is just going to go dark and cold, stars blinking out like candles on an interstellar birthday cake. And still others think that time itself will come to an end like an old man's watch that someone forgot to wind.

If forced to choose, I'd probably go with the last option. Not because it sounds like a barrel of laughs. But if it's all going to freeze like the last frame of an eighties movie, I think I could deal with it as long as I get to pick the right moment.

For example, I could be jumping off a cliff, locked in flight like a majestic Pegasus. Or I could be mid-hiccup, frozen in a deranged bodily spasm for all of time. Or maybe

I could just round up all the people I've disappointed in the last few months and issue one giant apology before it all goes still. I could shout it through a megaphone. I AM TESS FOWLER AND I HAVE MADE TERRIBLE MISTAKES! MY BAD! PLEASE ENJOY THE VOID!

And I guess if someone twisted my arm I might also opt for an eternal orgasm.

The Long Bang, if you will.

But the key here is that I want the power. I want to know when it's going to happen, and I want the ability to choose my last act when the time comes. Because, lately, I've been feeling like I don't have much control at all.

Dropping out of high school, as it turns out, is only mildly empowering. It *is* remarkably easy, though. All you have to do is wake up one morning and realize that you are failing the shit out of all of your classes, you have alienated most of the people who were once your friends, and you haven't really felt like a functioning human being for well over a month.

At which point, I recommend stealing the last emergency joint from your roommate's Mickey Mouse Band-Aid tin, walking to the two-lane highway that frames the entrance to Forever Friends Quaker Academy, and puffing away while saying good-bye to a place that almost felt like home for a while. Then I suggest you get in your Ford Festiva and blow town like a fugitive.

I neglected to wake my roommate, Emma, before I took off. She had snuck her boyfriend in again, and they were locked in a pornographic pretzel hold that defied the imagination. Seriously, they were like conjoined staircases in an Escher drawing, only naked and with more body hair.

So, instead of saying good-bye, I left her the twenty-five bucks I owed her, along with the rest of my orange ginger body mist, which she was always stealing anyway. Then I walked out and closed that door forever.

It sounds harsh but we never really had an honest conversation in our seven months together. Or even a fight. True, I was with her that time she didn't get her period and we watched clips of Teen Mom on YouTube and cried. But we weren't best friends. I'll never be her maid of honor, giving a tearful speech at her destination wedding. And I probably won't be giving her a kidney. At least not my favorite one.

But, for the last few months we slept two feet apart in a room the size of a prison cell. We shared a shower caddy. We held each other's hair when we got too drunk on Malibu and our barf smelled like suntan lotion. There's an intimacy in that.

I also declined to notify Elaine at Health Services, which I imagine will come to bite me squarely on the ass sooner or later. Elaine is the woman who has been talking to me about my "grieving process" for the last month or so. She is nice enough, I suppose, and she gives warm hugs. But when I see the pictures of her dog dressed in Halloween costumes, I am sad for her. It's like all the problems of girls like me have zapped her ability to have a real life. Now all she can do is worry and walk her spaniel.

Ultimately, though, I just couldn't deal with another one of her phone calls, where she asks such painfully earnest questions while not-so-secretly trying to ascertain whether or not I am going to off myself at her school. Well, I'm gone now, Elaine, so you don't need to worry about that anymore. I give you permission to be relieved. Have an extra drink at the staff happy hour this week. You deserve it.

I suppose it's worth mentioning here that I am squatting in my father's home at present, with no immediate plans to leave it. The house is a sagging two-bedroom in Minneapolis where he's lived since his marriage to my mother unraveled like a bad sweater. And I am back living in it for two reasons that I can discern.

The first is that it is only a morning's drive away from

my hippie school in Iowa, and that seemed like a good amount of time to be in a car with myself. The second is that my mother is currently on an extended retreat in India with her new boyfriend, Lars, practicing something called Ashtanga Yoga, which I take great delight in not picturing. So, I journeyed to Dad's bachelor rental, where he runs a funeral-planning business out of my former bedroom.

Yes, you read that correctly.

For the last few years, my father has been trying to find exciting new angles in the Death business. He has been doing this despite any real training and a steady lack of encouragement from nearly everyone he knows.

There are still piles of unfinished coffins in the garage from his first attempt at "artisanal caskets." And now that he's trying to work as a funeral planner, there are pamphlets all over my old bedroom that say "Plan for the Party of Your Life!" (Which really means your DEATH. Surprise!)

This is not new behavior from him, unfortunately, and it's very much part of the reason we don't talk too often anymore. If I had to be more specific, I would say that most of the reason we don't talk is the fact that he drained a college fund in my name to cover costs for another of his "ventures." That one was a mobile spa unit he could drive to the homes of the elderly to perform hot stone massages on their seminude bodies in their driveways. Sweet idea, Dad. How did that fail to take off?

He was, of course, going to pay the money "right back!" But somehow he just ended up borrowing more from my mom . . . without asking her. Yet, despite all this, I called him last night in a moment of weakness. Or desperation. Or maybe just to give him fair warning about my ruined life.

Anyway, when I got through, I caught him on a beach in Nantucket, where I immediately heard what sounded like fireworks launching into the night sky.

"Duncan Fowler!" he shouted over a prolonged screech.

"Dad?"

"Hello? This is DUNCAN!"

"DAD. THIS IS TESS!"

The screech came to an end.

"Tess," he said. "What's wrong?"

I couldn't blame him for asking. The only time he ever got a call from me was when something was going horribly.

"Nothing," I lied. "Nothing is going horribly."

A deafening explosion stepped on my line.

"What?" he said.

"NOTHING IS WRONG!" I said. "EVERYTHING IS PERFECT!"

Silence.

"Dad," I said. "What the hell is going on? It sounds like an air raid over there."

"I'll be honest." He sighed. "You haven't caught me at the best time, kid."

I couldn't remember a time when I had.

"I just have to tell you one thing," I said. "I'll be quick."

I took a breath and made sure another boom wasn't coming.

"I'm quitting," I said.

I didn't wait for him to respond.

"I gave up. On school. I'm quitting and coming home, probably forever. I hope that's cool with you."

I expected a gasp. Or at very least a sigh. All I got was another crackle in the air.

"Dad?"

"I'm sorry," he said. "I lost you for a minute. Did you say something?"

I closed my eyes and mouthed a few f-bombs.

"Forgive me, Tess," he said. "The ceremony isn't going so great here. The rockets just went off ahead of schedule and people are kind of freaking."

"Wait a minute. Rockets? What are you talking about?"

"They were supposed to go off at twelve, but it's only

eleven thirty. I'm not sure why that's such a big deal, but apparently Zebulon was born just after midnight. . . ."

"Who is *Zebulon*?" I asked.

I both did and did not want to know.

"A Borzoi!" he said. "Beautiful dog. At least, he was. He's been through a cremulator now, poor guy. He belonged to a famous science fiction writer. Thus, the rockets. And the name Zebulon, I guess. He's being launched as we speak. It's really quite—"

Another staccato of bursts.

"Hold on. You're doing dog funerals now?"

"Well," he said, "this is technically a *life celebration*, but yeah. It's sort of an untapped market. Anyway, I'm kind of busy. And it's almost exam time for you, right? What do they have you doing at that school, birthing a calf?"

For a moment, I considered telling him the truth. I considered telling him that I was no longer learning things at the expensive private high school where my mom had sent me to "self-actualize," and "build community." I considered telling him I was, instead, at his house in Minneapolis, eating out of his sad bachelor fridge and getting ready to sleep in my old room—which now looked like a cross between a home accountant's office and a prostitute's garret—but then I heard some shouts from a faraway crowd.

"Oh crap," he said. "Not good. The smoke is blowing back toward the beach. I need to move the old people. We'll talk about this later, okay, Tessie?"

And then, just like that, he was gone.

So, I closed my eyes and lay back on the bed.

It was and still is a single mattress bought for a smaller me. A smaller me who peed the bed well into her sixth year and was afraid of the dark until fifteen when she discovered Xanax and droning guitars. I hadn't slept on it in almost a year until last night. Now the springs are shot and the mattress dips in the middle like a hammock. But, still, I tried to find sleep in the office of death.

It was too quiet, though. I had been conditioned by Quaker school, and now I needed the sound of shouts echoing down the residence hall, and the rustles and shuffles of Emma and her boyfriend trying to have considerate sex across the room when they thought I was sleeping. I needed the sounds of other people, whatever those might be. Reminders that I wasn't completely alone.

So my attempt at shut-eye didn't last too long. And instead of making some tea, or meditating, I got up and I sent a long message to the Facebook account of a person who no longer exists.

The vacant person's name is Jonah.

His account is vacant because he's not alive anymore.

Still, despite his un-aliveness, I sent my message to him. I told him about trying to go to bed in a room full of eerily upbeat death brochures. I told him about a new iPhone app that identified constellations when you point it at the night sky. I told him I missed his late night texts, his rambling e-mails, and the sound of his laughter on my voice mail. And I told him that I was home, but it didn't feel like home anymore.

I also told him that everything happening to me was entirely his fault.

That if I hadn't known him, hadn't fallen for him against my better judgment, none of this would be occurring. I wouldn't be wearing the same clothes I wore yesterday. I wouldn't be lying on my sagging mattress from sixth grade, unable to move. I wouldn't be a high school dropout. And I wouldn't be barely holding in the full-body heartache that threatened to swallow me whole whenever I looked at his profile picture.

Then I waited two hours for a response that I knew would never come.

Which finally leads me to everything that happened this

morning, and the story I intended to tell in the first place before I began talking about other doomed things like the universe and Zebulon the rocket dog.

So, I'd like to give this another try, if you don't mind. My English teacher, Mr. Barthold, once told me that I need to "trust the process," when crafting a piece of writing, and that "the essential truth is a slippery thing."

Duly noted, Mr. B. Even though you are an embittered man clinging to a single published novel like a participation trophy, you sounded genuine when you said this. So I shall heed your advice and trust the process. Okay?

Fantastic.

Here goes.

2

I was sitting on the hardwood floor of the guest room in my underwear when I knew suddenly that I needed to go down to the lake. Well, first I needed to get dressed. Then I needed to go outside and walk to the lake. I had been up for about an hour hitting Reload on my browser, waiting, as usual, for a message from the void, when I finally just got up and got dressed. Then I slipped into the streets of Minneapolis with my computer under my arm.

Nobody was out. It was too early, even for Midwesterners. So, I wandered down the middle of the road toward the small lake at the bottom of the hill, where rich people pay a million dollars to stare at water. And while I walked, I tried to be honest with myself about the recent trajectory of my grief.

The truth is I had never lost anyone before. At least nobody my own age. I wasn't sure what it was supposed to feel like in normal circumstances, let alone my "not normal at all" circumstances. Let's just say there were complicating factors. Namely: Jonah and I had only met in person one time.

For about five hours.

Did I forget to mention that?

"Boyfriend of the Internet!" Emma had called him once, "BF 2.0."

And she wasn't wrong. We had mostly engaged via the device currently under my armpit. E-mail. Facebook. Texting. Etc. And now that he was gone, his death felt both like an absence and not. It was true he had never really been here to begin with. Only once did I see him looking at me from across the room with his beguiling gray-blue eyes, or smiling at me with that one crooked incisor that made him look a little devious when he was just trying to be charming. But *something* had been here.

Something I couldn't bring back.

And in the last two weeks, I had actually been sending him more messages than ever before. Even though I knew he couldn't respond, I checked my in-box fifty times a day. Click. Reload. Click. Reload. I was sure he would write eventually and tell me it was all a hoax. *I'm not dead. I'm alive! It was all a very funny joke on you by me! Ha-ha!* But that never happened, and I was starting to scare myself a little. So in these last few moments before first light, it finally became clear to me what I must do.

I must commit my two-thousand-dollar personal computer to the depths of the lake at the bottom of the hill.

Once upon a time, before I knew what clinical depression was, I had cross-country skied over this lake. It was a hazy memory, but a nice one. I shuffled over the snow-covered surface at night by the light of candles gleaming in hollowed-out ice blocks. My parents were still together back then and they stood by my side, helping me along. At the finish line there were ice pyramids stacked on the lake like tombs for frozen pharaohs.

Now, of course, the lake was wholly thawed, but it was the idea of the frozen surface that pulled at me. Come winter, my computer would have an icy burial mound, all my communications with Jonah encased inside.

As I walked toward the lake, though, I couldn't stop thinking about the fact that if things had been different, I might be with him right now instead of doing this. All spring, we had been building toward a second meeting. We texted about it every day, trading job listings at all hours, convinced we could work at the same place after school was through.

Anywhere would do. The more ridiculous the better.

It would make a good story for our grandchildren, Jonah said. And a bizarre new beginning to our relationship. So we started a list and said yes to everything. A clowning camp in Alaska? Sure. An arts initiative at a women's prison in Oklahoma? Why not? A summer at sea on the Bosporus Strait? Sign me up!

Anytime we saw summer work for teenagers, no matter how strange, we sent it to the other. It became a code between us. A declaration of our desire to unite as walking, talking actual people. To be together the way everyone else was.

I'd write:

> **On a scale of 1 to 10, how do you feel about inseminating salmon eggs?**

And he'd write back:

> **Nine! Who's going to inseminate them if not us?**

Then, an hour later he'd write:

> **Cooks needed at nudist colony in Spokane. Nightly wiener roast?**

After a while, however, I noticed that I was the only one sending jobs.

> You down for organic beet farming?
> We could be the Beet Generation!
> Hahahahahahahaha (punches self
> in face).

Or simply:

> Rodeo clowns?

And nothing would come back.

Not even that emoji he was so fond of, the one with the smiley face sticking its tongue out. The one I'd always assumed meant "You are cute and funny and clever and did I mention cute?" but now I think probably meant "I am not actually engaging with you, Tess Fowler. This stupid grinning face is a BS substitute for real communication."

I passed the top of the hill and felt the ground beneath me begin to slant. The far bank of the lake came into view. It wasn't quite dawn yet, but the clouds were just beginning to glow a buttery yellow. And, seemingly against my will, I began to narrate to Jonah about what was happening.

In my head, I saw the little blinking cursor on my e-mail's chat function. Then I saw my usual string of text starting to fill it in one word at a time, like it had so often.

Me: **Things I'm seeing without you:**

This was a game we played on occasion, looking out the

windows of our respective rooms, half a country away, and just describing what we saw. If we were doing it simultaneously, it was possible, Jonah said, to be in two worlds at once.

He was cheesy like that.

Me: **Steam coming off the pavement. Motion detector lights popping on and off like little lightning flashes.**

Me: **Rabbits. Baby rabbits? How can you tell a baby rabbit from a small adult rabbit? Are small rabbits confused for babies in the rabbit world? Is it humiliating?**

A couple of times we tried the game with video chat, pointing our laptop cameras out the window, actually seeing what the other saw, but it wasn't the same. It was always better with words. Translating the world for each other.

Me: **Automatic sprinkler systems. Fountains. A few covered pools in backyards.**

At the bottom of the hill, I crossed the road to the lip of the path around the shore.

Me: **The lake. Looked so big to me when I was a kid. Now it's just a little guy. An oversize swimming pool with fish. So clear today. A lone rower is out. Is she trying for a moment's peace before her crappy day begins? Is she training for something? Who are you, lady rower? Why are you working so hard? You have badass arms.**

In the days after he was gone, I could tell immediately that something had shifted. At some point, I didn't know when, life had only started to feel real when I wrote to him about it. I was a better, funnier version of myself when I told him things. Life was manageable that way. My brain was manageable. Now, the days I was living felt robbed of something, and I needed to find a way to get it back or things were going to get really, really bad.

Me: The steps of the wooden dock. The green algae on the water. The rower looking at me through reflective sunglasses. The cool morning breeze that kicks up. And then the full light of the sun finding its way over the horizon.

Now the sky is blue-ing and the water is blue-ing. The computer in my hands. So smooth and metallic. Me cocking back my arms. The rower looking confused, a hand to her head like a scout's as she battles the sunlight.

A ripple moves over the surface of the lake. My computer whipping through the air like a square Frisbee, and landing, where it splashes, dies, and sinks into the murky depths with only the smallest of air bubbles. The way my shoes look running down the dock toward the water. The moment where I leap above the water and see it underneath me like a shiny marble floor.

A shout from the rower. The cold water, cloudy with eyes

open. Total dark with eyes closed. My arms pushing through the lake water in slow motion. The weeds against my shins. Then the blinding white sun when I kick my legs and break to the surface, screaming so loud that my lungs feel like they might combust.

This is it.

What I'm seeing without you.

3

The only time I met him in person, he had a patchy teenage beard.

It hid his top lip and made his expressions hard to read. It also made him look extra boyish—a kid playing grown-up—when I saw him on the porch of the farmhouse last fall. We were both at a party thrown by college kids from the nearby university. They lived right by my school in a rundown house, complete with a chicken coop and a rusty grain bin.

"Trust farmers," some of the girls called them. They were rich kids playing good country folk, all the way down to the chewing tobacco and seed caps. It wasn't so different from what we were doing at Quaker school, but at least we knew we were ridiculous. These guys took it super seriously. They wore overalls and bandannas. They spoke in reverent tones of keeping bees.

And yet:

I snuck out and went to their party. I did this because I was lonely and I wanted to drink beer without paying for it. One of my classmates, a kid named Satchel, told me about the party in art class. "There's going to be apple bobbing!" he said with such a rapturous look of joy on his face, anyone might have thought he was talking about skydiving into Stonehenge. And I wondered: Could anyone over the age of eight actually be that excited about dunking their head in a tub of cold water?

I received my answer upon arriving. One of the first things I saw was a gaggle of bearded boys submerging their faces into an old basin. There seemed to be some kind of drinking element worked in, too—shots of whiskey pre- or post-bob—but I couldn't quite understand, so I walked past them and spent the next hour filling and refilling my plastic red cup from the barn keg.

"Do you know what kind of beer this is?" a girl in line asked me at one point. "Free," I told her.

I saw Jonah right around the time I left the land of buzzed for the uncertain waters of Drunk-as-Hell. It's hard to imagine our meeting in any other way. Since arriving at Quaker school in the fall, I had been experiencing some immobilizing social anxiety for the first time. High school in New York (where I spent the year before living with my mom) hadn't been a cakewalk, but I had a few friends.

Gradually, I'd learned to dole out my "real" personality in small, safe doses to avoid scaring people away. Since I'd been here, however, I had felt myself pulling back, saying things in my head instead of out loud. Smiling less. I got tension headaches after class sometimes. It was odd, and inexplicable, and the only cure seemed to be the newly discovered one of alcohol.

I was standing on the porch of the farmhouse, feeling some inexact measure of shame and longing, when I saw a farmer boy lurking near the tub used for apple bobbing. He peered inside at the bitten red apples, an odd half smile on his lips, and I felt a quick welling of anger.

"Can you please explain it to me!" I shouted.

The guy turned around, surprised, but too far away to see clearly.

"I'm sorry?" he said.

He had a low voice, and there was a surprising warmth to it. It nearly halted my momentum. But my tongue had been loosened, and its lashing was not to be denied!

"What is with the farm fetish?" I said. "I really want to know."

I stepped closer to him. He didn't speak. Instead, he adjusted his glasses.

"I mean: I get the desire for authenticity. We all want to feel connected to something real, the loamy dirt or whatever. But pretending you're in *The Grapes of Wrath* when you're actually a Media Studies major from Boston is not the answer, my friend. You're not Amish! You're not raising a barn tomorrow! Just give it up, okay?"

I could have said more. I very much wanted to say more. After speaking no more than a word or two the entire evening, it felt amazing just to talk again. Unfortunately, right after I spoke my last word, I realized that I was incredibly nauseous. The feeling hit me like a sucker punch, and before I could excuse myself, I was already launching into a wobbling sprint to the edge of the porch.

Then I was vomiting in the bushes.

Continuously. Heaving and hiccupping away, like a deranged beat-boxer while strangers watched in horror. In no time, I had emptied everything from my body. My entire being, I'm pretty sure, was now in the shrubbery. My legs teetered beneath me, but instead of tipping off the porch, a hand appeared on my side, holding me in place.

"Come on," said the hand. "This way."

I followed the trust farmer attached to the hand. It seemed, suddenly, like the right thing to do. I followed him to the kitchen where I took little sips from a tumbler of cool water. Glorious little tumbler sips. I swished the water in my mouth and spit it in the sink like a boxer, tears streaking down my burning cheeks (when exactly had I started to cry?). My farmer led me to a couch and had me lie down with a foot on the floor to keep the room from spinning. Just one foot. Then he spoke in his low voice:

"I'm Jonah, by the way. I don't live here."

I was not technically drunk anymore. Nor was I technically sober. I was in a place between the two that didn't leave much padding between thought and speech.

"But, you have a beard!" I said.

He smiled.

"I do have one of those. I just thought I'd try it. It seemed collegey."

I could see him more clearly in the light of the living room, and I could tell within seconds that he would look ten times better without facial hair. It looked like there was a strong chin under there.

"Do you go to the university?"

He shook his head.

"I'm from Syracuse. But I go to school in Boston," he said. "I came here to visit a friend from high school. But

I don't think we're friends anymore. It's too bad. We used to be close. It's hard to find that, you know? Do you want more water?"

But I was not listening. Not really. I was watching his face. His eyes were a little squinty beneath a pair of oversize glasses. But they were a lovely gray with blue around the pupils. His nose wasn't as prominent as I usually liked, but it wasn't *un-prominent*. And his tangle of blond hair was just messy enough. Was he handsome? Probably he was. It always took me too long to decide.

"Ha," I said finally.

"What?"

"You're a Media Studies major from Boston."

"I don't know what Media Studies is."

"Oh."

"I do things with computers," he said.

"Nerdy things?"

"Yeah. Probably. Most things I do are nerdy."

I nodded.

"It's far away," I heard myself saying.

"What's that?"

"Boston. It's far."

"I guess that's true."

My head was nodding. Drooping actually. I was drifting

off. Now that I was empty, my body was ready to be done with this night.

"Dammit," I said. "I'd like to keep talking to you, Jonah. There is something about your voice that is really god-damned peaceful, but I guess I'm going to sleep now. You know how it is."

He was quiet a moment then motioned toward my couch.

"Actually, that's where I'm supposed to sleep," he said.

And again, I spoke without thinking.

"We can share it if you want," I said. "But I'm not getting up. That's my best offer."

I closed my eyes and beneath my lids there were pictures, bursts of light zooming here and there. It took Jonah maybe a minute or so to decide, but eventually he came over and sat down beside me. He smelled like laundry detergent and a long-ago spritz of cologne. He lay down. I leaned my head on his chest and he held absolutely still. I felt warm all over my body.

In the movie version of this scene, we make out feverishly. Then we wake in each other's arms like Italian teenagers from that old Zeffirelli movie we watched in AP English. But this wasn't Shakespeare. We were not in Verona. We were in Iowa at a fake farmhouse full of passed-out undergraduates and imitation Quakers.

So, instead, I woke up the next afternoon with a catastrophic hangover, a fresh dose of hell to pay at school, and an e-mail address written on a gas station receipt that read: "Boston is very far away. The Internet is not."

4

The rower's name was Grace.

Remember her?

She was staring at me from across my dad's kitchen table.

She was tan and fortyish and flushed from the sun, and there was a white spot of zinc on her nose that looked like yogurt. She had freckles and she wore a formfitting rowing suit that showed some serious cleavage.

And me? I wore a ratty orange towel draped over a T-shirt that said: *Shave the Whales*, which I thought was hilarious when I bought it at Hot Topic in the ninth grade. It was soaked in stagnant lake water.

We had been in exactly these positions for the last half hour, ever since Grace had hoisted me from the freezing lake, rowed me to the shore, and driven me back home to wait for my father. In this time, which felt very long, but was probably very short, we had exchanged exactly six sentences. Actually, "exchange" probably isn't the right word.

She had spoken five of these sentences, which were, in order:

1) Oh my God!
2) What were you doing jumping like that?
3) Seriously, are you okay?
4) I'm Grace.
5) Where do you live?

I had spoken one sentence, which was:

1) Up the hill with my dad.

And since then we had reached a bit of an impasse.

Outside in the driveway I could see Grace's Jeep with her small boat mounted on top. A *scull*. The word had come to me out of nowhere while I was gliding to the shore, sunlight burning through my eyelids. *I am in a scull,* I thought. *I am being rowed in a scull.* It was sleek and red, and it was currently pointing toward the house like an accusing finger.

I knew it was my job to say things now, to give Grace some sense of the reasoning for my crazed leap lake-ward, but I couldn't. I wasn't even sure I could form words. The only thing I knew was that I wanted desperately for this woman to leave, and at the same time, I wanted her to stay exactly where she was.

I had no idea when my father would be back. Most of his

jobs, when he had them, were just a day or two long. But who knew, maybe a gerbil had a stroke and he was urgently needed somewhere in Maine. In which case, Grace and I would be sitting here looking at each other for the next few hundred hours.

Who would be the first to crack, I wondered. I imagined she must have a job, a family. Anyone who looked so tan and put-together must have these things. She probably had a doting husband who did something with people's endocrine systems while she pursued her love for . . . antique lighting fixtures? She would have to give in eventually. She had a life to return to.

Which made one of us.

Our staring contest, however, was never given a chance to run its course. This is because just when I was getting the upper hand, I heard the screen door rattle in its frame. Then I heard my father's unmistakable too-loud voice echo through the hallway.

"Tessie!" he shouted. "Is that you?"

He shuffled into the living room, slamming the door closed behind him.

"Tessie," he boomed. "Are you home? Whose car is that outside? It's parked in my spot!"

I could almost see through his eyes as he passed his drab

furniture. Did he even notice it anymore? The cracked coffee table. The stained couch. The wallpaper in the hall, starting to peel. Finally, he appeared in the doorway to the kitchen where he stopped and remained still for what must have been at least ten seconds. He looked from me to Grace the Rower, both of us silent.

"Okay," he said eventually. "Anyone want to let me know what's going on?"

I glanced up at his face, which had always been young and handsome compared to the faces of other dads. He had me when he was just nineteen. Today, however, he looked a little tired. His wide brown eyes were red-rimmed. And his long hair, which was just starting to go gray, glittered with sand. He wore a black suit and in his right hand, he held his favorite tote bag, which read: DEATH: IT'S A LIVING.

"Who are you?" he asked Grace. Then he turned back to me and said: "Tessie, what's happening?"

I wasn't yet able to speak. And neither was Grace.

I should add here that middle-aged women always seem to have the hots for my dad. They think he's hunky in a bohemian sort of way. Before he became such a divorced sad sack, waitresses flirted with him shamelessly when we went out to dinner. Sometimes right in front of my mom, who found the whole thing confounding. "They don't have to watch you floss," she said once. Anyway, sitting there in the kitchen, I felt like I could already see Grace sizing him up.

"I'm Grace," she said now, "and I am in your kitchen because I rescued your daughter from the lake this morning."

"The lake?" said my dad, like it was a place he'd never heard of.

"The one at the foot of the hill," said Grace. "The one your daughter jumped in."

I felt my face warming.

"Oh Christ," I said. "She didn't *rescue* me."

I avoided eye contact with Grace, but I could feel her watching me.

"I'm sorry," she said. "You weren't flailing around in the lake, screaming? That's not what was happening when I found you?"

My dad looked around the kitchen, as if searching out more evidence.

"Tess," he said, "I think I'm missing something here. Why are you home from school? And why were you in the lake with your clothes on this morning?"

My cheeks felt hot. My heart was beating in my ears.

"I was doing my morning row," said Grace, "earlier than usual, and I saw her jump. It looked . . ."

She stared at me.

"It looked like she was going to drown or something. I thought maybe she was trying to . . ."

I stood up and took a step toward Grace, holding tears at bay.

"I wasn't trying to do anything," I said. "I didn't need to be rescued by your stupid little boat that looks like a dildo. It was a purification ritual! It was for my soul! You ruined it. And now you can leave. Dad, I'm sorry for the trouble. I'd like her to go now, please."

But my father was stuck in place. His eyes were locked on Grace. And for some reason, the fact that he was haplessly looking at this woman and not at me, his soaked and half-crazed daughter, pushed me over the edge. I felt my jaw clench, and when I spoke I hardly knew what I was saying.

"Dad," I said. "Quit staring at the boat lady! Grace, I don't need a babysitter anymore. Thanks for nothing. I'll see you all in hell."

And at that, I stalked out of the room like a teenage drama queen, my shoes squelching on the varnished wood. But as

I walked up the stairs, I risked a single look back and met eyes one last time with Grace. And I was surprised to see that the look on her face wasn't angry. It didn't even seem annoyed. Instead, there was just a knowing stare that made me turn away.

Upstairs, I noticed that the taste of lake water was still in my mouth. It was brackish and sour, like fish had been peeing in it since the dawn of time. I remembered floating in the lake and looking up. The clouds had been so close, like they were right on top of me. I didn't feel any time passing before Grace reached out and grabbed me. She had been shouting, but, at first, I couldn't hear it. My ears were plugged with water and everything sounded miles away.

"I'm still a little unsure . . ."

I heard my father's voice from the window near my bed. He was down in the driveway. I inched toward the window and cracked it open.

". . . never been great with authority. She got kicked out of summer camp once for inciting a riot. I'm sure she'll be—"

"No," said Grace, interrupting him.

I watched her stand with perfect posture in the driveway.

"No?" Dad said.

"I don't think she'll be fine," she said.

She walked closer to him.

"I'm not sure exactly what your daughter was doing this morning, but it didn't seem fine to me. It seemed very strange. When I pulled her out of the water, I couldn't get her to talk to me for ten minutes. She was freezing cold and she was crying. I think she might need some help."

The last word, and all that it implied, seemed to shock my father. He ran his hand through his hair.

"I should go," she said. "But do me a favor."

"What's that?" he said.

"Wake up. Your daughter needs you."

I watched her walk to her Jeep. I could just make out the bumper stickers. MY OTHER CAR IS A BIKE, read one. Another said, COMPOST HAPPENS. A larger one read simply: GREENER PASTURES.

Grace rolled down her window and turned on the ignition. My father's mouth was slack. Grace put the Jeep into gear, backed out of the driveway, and coasted down the road with her windows open. I watched her hair swirl around in the wind. And even after her car was out of sight, blocked by a neighbor's hedge, I could still see her red and white boat cutting a wake through the air.

5

Dear Jonah,

If you want the world to wonder if you have completely lost your shit, your best bet is to jump into a lake fully clothed.

That will get the job done for you pretty quick. It is also a great way to pick up a yeast infection, I've heard. I'll keep you updated on that front should new details become available (about my vagina).

Also, in case you are in some afterlife with Wi-Fi, I just thought you should know that my plan to cut off communication with you has not only failed but also resulted in a temporary lockdown. In fact, as I write this, I am currently in a state of exile in the office/guest room with only a few of my father's old *Playboy*s from the late 1980s to keep me company.

Briefly on that topic: I can't help mentioning that the amount of pubic hair I have seen in all of my existence has just gone up 80 percent in the last two hours. If I ever fall asleep again, I'll probably see it in my dreams.

Sorry. I'll move on.

You might be wondering, at this point, how I'm writing this at all. Especially since I told you (telepathically) I was chucking my computer into a lake. The answer is simple: I have temporarily commandeered my father's ancient PC, which looks suspiciously like the one I used to study "keyboarding" with Mrs. Hopkins in elementary school.

This computer is slow, but so is my brain, so we have found a kind of harmony. And now that I've found you again, maybe I should get to the point.

The point is this: When I haven't been having a series of mini panic attacks and/or staring at the wall, I've been thinking about an article you sent me once from a tech magazine.

This article was about death. A subject I've been thinking a lot about recently. And it projected that someday, in the not-too-distant future, we will all be able to upload our minds to computers as a form of life extension.

Basically we'll create an e-us, made of virtual DNA, and then, as long as the power doesn't run out, we will never

ever die. We will live on, alongside cat videos and the mean comments at the bottom of celebrity profiles.

At the time, this idea gave me the creeps so bad I had to watch videos of baby sloths falling off things for a half hour just to cleanse my thoughts. Now I'm not sure what to think. Maybe it's not so crazy to have a backup copy in case something happens to the original.

Maybe we're too careless with our first lives.

Let me state for the record that there are a number of questions I would like to ask you regarding your recent nonexistence. But to start listing all of them at this point would make this message at least a hundred pages longer. You see, you have effed me up in a number of significant ways. So, maybe I'll just ask this one:

Is this your backup copy, Jonah? Or am I truly just talking to myself?

Awaiting answer,
Tess

6

It was two in the morning when I finally gave up on sleep.

I had spent the last half hour listening to my father toss and turn in his huge bed across the hall. Another, kinder me might have tried to convince him that I wasn't completely losing my mind and that everything was going to be all right. Unfortunately, I am not another kinder me. I am just regular shitty me. And, even in the best of times, I have serious doubts about my own sanity and whether anything can ever truly be all right.

Also, my dad sleeps in the nude.

So, there you go.

It had taken him two full hours to come up to my room after Grace was gone. From what I could tell, he just sat in the driveway before that, talking on his phone. Probably with my mom. My back-assward life is the only thing that keeps them in contact anymore. If they didn't have my many problems to discuss they probably wouldn't even speak to each other.

Which is a little sad, particularly because my father has been slow to move on from the divorce, even though he squandered her money and generally acted like a selfish dick-nose during the latter part of their marriage.

Anyway, after Grace drove away, he eventually entered the house and walked upstairs one painstakingly slow step at a time. Then, as far as I could tell, he just stood outside my room, sighing. He didn't knock. He didn't try the knob. It was hard to tell, actually, how close to the door he was.

He had the habit, like a sulking child, of shutting down completely when something was wrong. It would be funny if it wasn't so infuriating. I felt the familiar anger this time, but it was quickly smothered beneath the sadness and shame I'd been nursing since I jumped in the lake. Eventually, after what seemed like a thousand hours, he stepped closer and cleared his throat.

"Um . . . Tessie?" he said.

He paused, waiting for a response. I provided none.

"So, I wish I could . . . um . . . understand what's going on here. But, since I don't have the faintest notion, and you aren't really being . . . um . . . generous with the details, I feel like I'm just kind of powerless, you know?"

I knew he was dying for a sign I was there, but I couldn't bring myself to give him one. I didn't know what to say.

"Here's the deal," he said after another substantial pause. "Your mother is not coming back early from India."

I thought I heard a sad laugh.

"She's there with . . . *him*. And I guess they're too busy bending their bodies into Lotus poses to be bothered with anything happening at home. Instead I've been given instructions. I'm supposed to drive you back to school tomorrow, and see that you finish the year. Your mother has made it clear that dropping out isn't an option in this family."

When I swung open the door, I nearly bashed my father in the face. As it turns out, he had been standing pretty close. He jumped back, and his expression looked somewhere between startled and angry.

"But you dropped out," I said.

"We're not talking about me," he said.

"Also we're not a family anymore," I said.

I looked at his hands. He appeared to be holding a plate of food.

"What's that?"

"I made you macaroni and cheese," he said. "With two cheese packets. The way you like it. Or, you used to, at least. You know . . . um . . . when you were a kid."

I stood looking at the plate for a moment, the pile of neon orange noodles. It looked both absurd and delicious, and for a moment I thought I might break down and let everything out.

Dad was always my confidant when I was a kid. Usually unemployed, he used to pick me up from school each day, searching me out in the crowd of tiny beings. On the long walks home, I'd narrate my entire day, and he'd nod as if every detail was fascinating. *Really? You fed the hamster an entire grape?* Then, if he was in a good mood, we'd stop to get Coke Slurpies from 7-Eleven and compare brain freezes.

But, we weren't really pals anymore. Now he was the guy who stole from me and ruined the later portion of my childhood with his self-obsession. I just reached out and grabbed the plate from his hands.

"Thanks," I mumbled.

He stood there blinking at me for another few seconds, then he spoke again.

"Tess, I have an opportunity," he said.

I looked around the hallway.

"What? Here?"

He shook his head.

"I got a phone call earlier. From out of state. I guess the guy hasn't heard about what happened in Nantucket yet with the . . . you know . . . dog explosion—"

"What kind of opportunity?" I interrupted.

"Well," he said. "The kind I specialize in."

I took a bite of macaroni.

"It's a job and, financially speaking, I need to take it."

He cleared his throat.

"So as far as I can tell, I have three options. One is to leave you behind and just go . . . do this job. But, after this morning, I just don't think that's going to be . . . um . . . possible. The second is to insist that your mom cancel her trip and come get you, but that doesn't seem to be realistic either. So then there's the last option, which is . . ."

"Who died?" I asked.

"I'm sorry?"

"You said it's a job, and your job involves the dead, right? So who died to make this golden opportunity possible?"

He chewed his bottom lip.

"Well," he said, "Sargent Bronson died."

"Who's Sargent Bronson?"

My father looked for a moment like he might break into a laugh. But when he spoke it was in a flat, even tone, as if what he said next was perfectly normal. And who knows, in his warped world, it probably was.

"Sergeant Bronson," he said, "is a racehorse."

7

After Jonah left me that note at the party last fall, we started to send e-mails. It was kind of quaint like that. We'd send long meandering updates on life at our respective schools, filled with boatloads of questions at the end for the other to answer. Sometimes an e-mail just full of answers would come back. Other times it was a series of texts, rapid-fire, one after the next.

So, while I went through each friendless day at Forever Friends, my phone would hum with his responses to questions I barely remembered asking.

Orange Soda. No question. It has the most grams of sugar per ounce.

Or:

Are you kidding me? Invisibility! It used to be flying, but then I went through puberty.

Or:

Cinemax at my friend's house. There was a movie on about

a sorority car wash. It only took five minutes for the first bikini to fall off. I never saw the sequel though. And I'm really concerned about the car wash. Did it stay in business?

Or, as the questions grew more personal:

Brooke, a girl I knew in fourth grade. She was diabetic and she had to carry around a little drink box of apple juice in case her blood sugar got too low. Watching her sip her drink box filled me with the most intense sensation of love I have ever felt. She kissed me under the slide, and then moved a year later. I don't know where she is now. I've never even looked her up. I just want her to exist in fourth grade forever.

And eventually:

I'd like to. Scratch that. I'd LOVE to, but I don't think I can afford the ticket right now. Don't worry, though. It will happen soon. So soon! There is no one I would rather see right now. No one.

The more I asked when he was coming to see me, the more I got answers like the one above. They were always positive, full of hope and enthusiasm, but each time, they completely shut down the idea of a visit. At first I thought he wanted to break up, but he didn't have the guts to tell me. Yet, if anything, his messages got more romantic.

Probably we should just get married. People in religious cults don't have a monopoly on marrying young. Anyone

46

can do it. I'm not going to officially ask you yet, but just think about it. Holy Matrimony. With me. Soon.

Til death do us part.

Is that really what he said at the end?

Yes it is.

I have the saved message to prove it.

And I was looking at this message, staring at those very words on my phone, when my father leaned over across the aisle of the airplane and removed the earbud from my ear. The drone of the engines filled the music's absence, and I was yanked back to the present. A present that included Dad and me on a chartered flight, speeding toward an unplanned horse funeral.

"Leroy Labelle," he said.

"Is that supposed to mean something to me?" I asked.

"He's the guy I'm working for. I thought you might want to know more about the job. You know, since you're coming."

"Thanks. I don't really."

I sat in a plush leather seat, feeling wholly detached from reality. The funeral was going to be in Ocala, Florida, the racehorse capital of the world. And while my interest in going was about the same as my interest in a pelvic exam, my options had become limited ever since my icy plunge.

Dad handed me a cell phone and pressed play on a voice

mail. And before I could give it back, a voice that couldn't have sounded more Southern came through the speaker.

"Mr. Fowler, this is Leroy Labelle phoning you. Got your information by way of your website. I wonder if we might have ourselves a talk sometime today or tomorrow in regards to a great loss my family has suffered . . . wait . . . oh Goddamnit I seem to have pressed a . . . I don't use this touch screen very often . . . I tried that . . ."

(Incoherent swearing)

"Okay . . . I'm back. I'll be honest with you, Fowler. Not more than a nickel's worth of preparations have been made for this thing. Usually we don't go too gaga over a dead animal around here, but I guess we underestimated just how we'd feel about our boy Sarge."

I thought I heard a sniffle.

"He was a hell of a Thoroughbred and the best damn stud we've ever had. He deserves a heck of a send-off. Now, I heard you specialize in this sort of thing, so I hope you can work quickly. I've got seventy-two hours to get this body in the ground before I'm in legal trouble. My only question to you is: How soon can you get down here?"

When the voice mail was over, my dad flipped through some pictures on his phone and handed it back to me. Then I found myself staring into the pained, obsidian eyes of a blue roan horse. A now extinct blue roan horse. Its eyes were so black it was unnerving. My dad must have caught me staring.

"They have cable," he said. "You can stay in the house the whole time and watch those terrible reality shows you like. I don't care."

"You already told me about the cable," I said.

"Well, I'm telling you again. It could be relaxing. Like a spa."

I shot him a look that I hoped said: *Do not make this horse funeral sound like a vacation because we both know that is a load.* We sat quietly next to each other for the next few minutes. Finally, he leaned over again and said:

"I got my GED."

"What?" I said.

"You said I dropped out of high school. That's not really true. I got my GED. It was important to me. I'm proud of it."

I stared at him.

"I remember," I said finally. "Mom was so happy for you."

He didn't break eye contact.

"Eventually, you have to talk to me about what's going on," he said.

Maybe that's true, I thought, *but not right now*. So, I put my earbud back in and picked up the newspaper from the seat back in front of me. It was from

Ocala and all the articles inside were horse-related.

There was a roundup of recent victors in national races, profiles about historic farms, and, on the very front page, there was a long story about an outbreak of equine herpes. I read the whole thing, just to keep myself distracted.

My takeaway: Do not get equine herpes.

When we landed, the ride to Leroy's farm was long and slow. Our driver, Skip, whose head looked slightly too large for his body, took us down winding country roads bordered by wooden fences and historic horse barns. All around, there were brushed, shining horses galloping across sun-kissed meadows. They looked like they were auditioning for a nine-year-old girl's wall calendar.

"You loved horses when you were little," my dad said.

I watched a glassy-eyed Appaloosa follow the progress of our car.

Dad continued: "I spent hours watching that show with you. The one about the rainbow ponies."

"You used to watch *My Little Pony* with me?" I asked. "Why did you subject yourself to that?"

He shrugged and looked out the window.

"I wanted to spend time with you. It was what you liked to do."

We were silent after that.

Until Skip the Driver began to speak.

"As you can see," he said, "we're approaching Stoneshire Estates."

I looked in the mirror and found some life in his eyes. It was like someone had just plunked a quarter in him.

"Located in the famed Golden Corridor of Ocala," he began, "this lush and opulent acreage is proof enough that Ocala is the true Horse Capital of the US."

A huge metal gate slid open, and our car entered a white gravel path. Inside was a secret garden overflowing with wildflowers.

"This is all thanks to the stewardship of Mr. Leroy Labelle, a second-generation Florida horseman with an enduring vision and an irrepressible spirit!"

I hoped Skip got paid a lot of money to say these things because he sounded like a bit of an asshole. The car was reaching the end of the path, and we were approaching a New England–style home, painted the color of fresh egg yolk. Surrounding it was a canopy of moss-draped oak trees.

As soon as we stepped out of the car, a man began walking toward us, dressed in a butterscotch-colored suit. He wore a pink dress shirt beneath the jacket and a pair of shimmering gold cuff links at his wrists. My first thought was: What is Willy Wonka doing on a horse farm? Of course, it was Leroy.

"There he is!" he shouted. "The man of the hour!"

He walked right past me and squeezed my dad's hand in a desperate grip. He smiled and sucked his teeth. I got out of the car.

"This must be your daughter!" he said, and clapped his hands together. "Welcome to Stoneshire! Welcome to horse country! If God didn't make this place, then who did? That's what I want you to tell me, young lady."

I looked over the house and the lush lawn surrounding it.

"Sorry for your loss. Apparently, I used to be really into ponies," I said.

Leroy blinked. He had a sizable mustache. It twitched.

"Yes," he said softly. "Of course. Thank you, sweetheart."

He turned back to my dad.

"Skip will take your bags, and he'll show the young lady around. But before we get started on the planning, there's something we need to do. There can be no inspiration without it."

"Do you want to tell me more about Sarge?" my father asked.

"No," said Leroy. "I want you to see his body."

8

When I got to my room, Skip waited outside my door for a half hour straight asking me to come out for a tour. He had been ordered to show me around pony town, and he wouldn't take no for an answer. I could only stall him by pretending I didn't know what to wear.

"Are you done yet?" he asked for the fifth time.

"No," I said. "I'm totally naked. Go away."

"You've already been in there twenty-five minutes."

"I'm giving myself a Brazilian," I said.

He turned the handle and opened the door.

"I could have been totally naked," I said.

"But you aren't."

"But I could have been. . . ."

"C'mon," he said. "The golf cart's waiting."

And it was. Just sitting there, puttering away as golf carts do. So we got in and sped over the gravel road. And Skip started up right where he left off.

"Stoneshire has had just about every breed of horse you could imagine at one time or another. We've had Paso Finos, Quarter horses, Arabians. Warmbloods. Every kind of horse. And we've bred 'em all!"

Now that I was next to him, Skip seemed younger than he did earlier, maybe closer to my age than I first thought. And he wasn't terrible looking actually. I hadn't noticed his masculine jaw at first. It was strong and coated in a light amount of stubble. I could imagine him nursing a calf back to health with a baby bottle before going inside to have wholly unselfconscious sex with a beautiful woman. And the sex would definitely make a baby. A stupid, angelic baby.

"This right here is the Thoroughbred training track. This is where we get our young horses in shape and teach 'em to race. Our youngbloods are broken to ride in September, and they can gallop a mile by December. You can bet on it!"

The problem with Skip, I decided, was that he said things. Also, he probably believed that the world was a beautiful place. But I could forgive him that if he would just stop speaking. If you could just watch him smile and frown as he drove various vehicles around, he might be okay.

"They got this machine in there called a vibration plate.

Wiggles around like crazy to get the circulation going in a horse's legs. It's hard to get them to stand on . . ."

I don't care, I thought. *I don't care about this at all.*

Skip hit the breaks, and the cart bucked to a stop. I jolted forward in my seat.

"Well, jeez," he said, "if you want me to stop bending your ear, you could be a little nicer about it."

I covered my mouth with my palm.

"Shit," I said. "Did I say that out loud?"

Skip gave me a puzzled look.

"Yes," he said. "You definitely did."

It was hard to tell if he was hurt. He seemed more confused.

"Well, the cat's out of the bag, I guess," I said. "I don't really care about horse training or breeding or . . . any of this. I think it's sad and weird and sad. And if it didn't exist I would be fine. I might even be happier."

I was sweating all of a sudden, and breathing heavily, a couple of sure signs that I was about to welcome a passing spell of dread. The golf cart was idling in a field of old oaks. The horizon beyond was so endless it was a little frightening. I stepped off the cart and plopped down in the grass. I closed my eyes and took long deep breaths.

"Are you all right?" asked Skip.

"Just give me a minute," I said. "I just have to wait out the terror."

A cool breeze kicked up and blew my hair against my cheeks.

"The what?"

"Terror." I said, "You know, the terror that humans feel. You don't have any weed do you?"

There was a long pause. I kept my eyes closed and my breath started to normalize a little. I pulled my hair into a ponytail and held it with a worn tie from my pocket.

"You don't feel good?" said Skip.

"Uh-huh," I murmured.

I heard the golf cart lurch forward behind me.

"Why didn't you say so," he said, "I got just the thing!"

"Is it medical-grade marijuana?"

"Nope."

"Then I don't want it."

The cart was coming closer to me. For a second, I wondered if he might hit me with it. Maybe that was his plan. To put me out of my misery.

"You don't even know what it is," he said.

The golf cart was chugging away right next to me now.

"I don't need to. I don't want *just the thing*," I said. "Whenever anyone says that, it's something terrible."

I finally opened my eyes and looked back at him, smiling in his miniature car.

"Come on, now," he said, "get in the dang cart. It's on the way back."

Fifteen minutes later we were speeding toward a barn. You couldn't spit without hitting a barn in this place, and the one we were approaching was the usual burnt red color. Skip pulled the cart up and parked it beneath an overhang. Then he got out and walked over to the entrance, waiting for me to follow.

When we stepped inside, I immediately breathed in that hay-and-pee smell of animal barns I'd walked through at the state fairs of my youth. I made my way down the middle of the stalls in a dim, dust-choked light. From around me came a few high-pitched whinnies and the occasional muffled snort. I found myself walking closer to Skip. The animals seemed to surround me on all sides.

"She's just down here," said Skip in a hushed voice that made me even more nervous. What the hell was in this barn?

"What the hell is in this barn?" I asked.

"Just relax," said Skip. "And see for yourself."

Skip came to a stop a few steps ahead of me and then just

stood there with his arms folded over his chest. I walked up and peered through the slats of a metal gate into a large stall strewn with fresh sawdust.

First I saw the sleeping body of a large mare, its chestnut coat expanding with breath. Then I heard a soft rustling, and out of the shadows of the far corner something small stirred and came forward.

It was a little creature. The tiniest horse I had ever seen.

"This is Linnie," said Skip. "Our newest foal. She was born just two days ago."

I slowly bent my knees and met the foal's eyes in a low squat.

"Linnie," I said.

The little horse took an unsteady step toward me, its bulbous black eyes searching my face. It was piebald, spattered with white across its forehead, black along the muzzle and ears. It walked closer to me, right up to the metal bars.

Without thinking much, I reached out my hand and unfolded my fingers. Linnie extended her muzzle and began to explore my hand with her lips. They were spongy and delicate, like a baby's, as they moved over my fingertips. I closed my eyes and waited for the clamp of teeth on my fingers.

"She doesn't have her milk teeth yet," said Skip. "She can't hurt you."

I looked over at him and found him grinning as usual. But, this smile seemed like more than his usual display of life satisfaction. He looked heartened. His faith in the beauty of the farm had persevered in the face of a crazy girl's skepticism.

I traced my fingers over the foal's forelock and then down her muzzle. Though I guess I had gone through a brief horse phase as a girl, I'd never had the desire to own one until now. I wanted to take this wobbly beanpole and smuggle her home in my duffel bag. That was all I needed to be happy. A pony.

I watched as Linnie gamboled around her stall, kicking up sawdust, eventually scrambling up her mother's flanks until she found a place to suckle.

"Just so you know," said Skip, behind me, "I have some weed, too. If that's what blows your hair back."

9

I've only been high a handful of times. I'm not going to claim stoner status like the boys at Quaker school who only put down the video game controller long enough to take a monster hit off a vaporizer. But as far as self-medicating goes, it helps take the edge off the anxiety sometimes. And it transforms microwave burritos into the food of the Gods. This time, though, I was in a little over my head.

Out behind the barn, I smoked a joint the size of a Pez dispenser with Skip. Then we took the golf cart joyriding. So there we were, racing over the vast pastures of the estate, laughing like idiots, when out on the fringes of the property, I saw a square aluminum building.

It looked like a mausoleum from the future. Something to house the cryogenically frozen heads of the Labelle family scions . . . or, as I realized immediately, their horses.

"Keep going!" I shouted. "Onward, Captain!"

As we drew closer, I saw two figures standing outside the

cube building. They popped into focus as my dad and Mr. Labelle. And it didn't look like they were getting along very well. Leroy's voice hitched itself to a current and I heard him shouting.

". . . because I'm pretty surprised!" he said, "I didn't expect any squeamishness from a man in your business, Fowler! What did you think I was going to do with him, let him rot? Have you ever smelled a decomposing animal? That's not the note we want to hit with Sarge's ceremony."

My father was slumped against the aluminum walls, massaging his temples. His ponytail was loose, and strands of gray-black hair danced in front of his eyes. He looked like he'd just seen a ghost. Which: okay, maybe he had.

"And you might be interested to know that I got an e-mail this morning," Leroy barked, "from a trusted colleague!"

We bounced over the minor bumps and dips in the paddock and braked to a stop. My father cocked his head in my direction.

"What kind of e-mail?" he asked Leroy.

"He sent me a little news story about a funeral in Nantucket."

"Oh," said my dad. "That."

Skip shot me a questioning look.

"Yes," said Leroy. "*That.* It sounded like a disastrous

funeral is what it sounded like. Like it couldn't have gone any worse if the devil himself had shown up, crapping fire!"

I looked at my father. I could already see him retreating, planning his escape route. I knew how his mind worked. When something started to go wrong, he was out of there. Gone.

I hopped out of the cart, a bit unsteady on my feet, and walked up to Leroy and my father. My head felt like it was full of helium. And it sounded like there were power lines crisscrossing my brain. I had no idea what I was going to say until I said:

"Everyone. I have just had a revelation."

They looked at me like I was from another planet.

"Tess," my dad said quietly, "you should head back and pack up your stuff. It's time to go."

A lone giggle escaped my mouth.

"Ha," I said. "You're all serious and everything."

I took a breath and tightened my face into a more pensive, sober look.

"Seriously," I said. "I have an idea. Hear me out."

I watched my dad steal a glance at Leroy. He didn't seem to be going anywhere. All eyes were now on me.

"Are you ready?" I said.

I waited a second or two and then I said: "Ponies."

There was a lengthy pause. My father stared into my pink eyes. No one seemed to find my idea as amazing as I did.

"I don't follow," Leroy said.

"Well," I said. "Okay. Not just ponies. But the horse babies. They're at the heart of this. Because they kind of symbolize the whole idea."

"What idea?" my dad said.

I looked at Leroy.

"This place is all about bloodlines, right?"

He just stared.

"Cycles of these amazing horses making more amazing horses. Then those horses make more horses, and everything just keeps cycling. Right?"

"Sure," Leroy conceded. "I suppose."

"And so I was thinking . . . that, in a way, these horses don't really die. I mean, they do die, everything dies, but there are all these little baby horses running around with Sarge's blood coursing through their little pony veins making them these incredible little racers! And if there's a horse that's truly astonishing, a one in a million horse, then this can happen forever. He can outrun the grave. So, we need to get all of Sarge's babies and we need to let them just run like hell, you know, to show that Sarge is not dead. He's still running. He's running so fast even right now. And he will always be running, you know? Always."

I took a deep breath and opened my eyes wide. Leroy watched me. His expression had not changed at all. He sucked his teeth. His mustache twitched slightly at the corners of his mouth.

"I think they should pull him in," he said.

"What?" said my father.

"We'll build Sarge a coffin and put it on a carriage. And all his children will pull him into the ceremony. Then we'll unhook them and let them run, like you said."

"I like it," I said. "They'll bring him home. To rest, right? Then they show that he still goes on."

Leroy nodded. He squinted off into the distance, as if he were imagining the whole thing, visualizing every detail. And when I looked, I could almost see it, too: the horse-drawn carriage, maybe a band playing, bold flags and tapestries hanging from the oaks while the procession marched underneath. Leroy tapped his foot. Then, eventually, he smiled.

"Okay, then," he said. "Let's get started."

10

Somehow, the horse funeral was a success.

By the light of a pink moon, they swung Sergeant Bronson's frozen body through the sky with a crane to get him from the freezer to his enormous coffin. The next day they thawed and embalmed him. Then they groomed him and made him look like a show horse. Midafternoon, a jazz marching band walked a procession route lined with yellow and white carnations. And when the time came, the trumpet call sounded, and the little horses were untethered one by one.

We all just stood there and watched them run as fast as they could over the pasture, disappearing until they were specks against the horizon. By the end of it all, Leroy had tears in his eyes. I saw him wipe them away on the sleeve of his butterscotch-colored jacket before plucking a nearby carnation for his lapel.

On the flight back, Dad seemed pleased.

I watched him as he stared out the window at the wispy clouds just beyond the wing, a calm smile on his face. No animals had blown up this time, and he had a big check in his pocket. How big, I couldn't tell you, but he kept touching it every once in a while to make sure it was still there.

"I probably didn't take the time to tell you, Tess," he said, "but thanks for your hard work the last couple days. That was, hands down, the best funeral I've done. And you're a big part of it."

"You're welcome," I said softly.

And, for the moment, I couldn't think of anything terrible to add. It's not like I felt like dancing or anything, but I was feeling slightly less awful. The funeral planning had been a helpful distraction. Also: Skip had given me his number before I left.

We weren't likely to see each other again, but it felt good to know I wasn't too far gone to attract a goofy-but-still-kind-of-hot cowboy. I couldn't help feeling a little guilty, though, for not turning him down flat. If things had happened differently, I would be with Jonah right now in a tiny cabin somewhere, making sustainable yurts with gifted children in the mountains.

"Leroy was impressed I let you have a say in my business."

My dad was talking again.

"He said his father never trusted him with the horses. Not until he was almost thirty. Can you believe that?"

"M-hmm," I said.

I opened my Facebook account and started to scroll through Jonah's pictures. The one, for instance, where he's on a camping trip, standing in a stream, his hair mussed from waking, an unlit cigarette hanging from his bottom lip. And the one where his arms are covered in scrabble tiles and he's caught mid-laugh on a dorm floor.

"Leroy doesn't have any kids. He doesn't know what he's going to do when he has to pass on his legacy."

I looked at the pictures people started posting after his death. A high school photo where he has long hair and he's crammed in a Porta Potti with four of his friends (complete with the caption "I'll always remember you like this, J. Much Love"). The first communion photo his aunt posted where he's wearing a white suit and looks a little like an R & B singer from the nineties. Her comment below said: "God got another angel today," as if he had actually died at the age of seven and not eighteen.

At first, it didn't register when I saw the message.

"He's worried when he dies, the horses will all go downhill. But that's what he liked about your idea. Maybe they'll be so strong they keep running. Even when he's gone, they'll keep running."

Not too many people contacted me on Facebook anymore. A couple of high school friends from New York, but mostly they texted if I heard from them at all. So it wasn't until I clicked on the icon and saw where the message was coming from, that my breath slowly left me.

There was Jonah's little face at the top right of the new message, which said:

I have to talk to you, Tess.

It's important.

"Tess," said my dad. "Did you hear me?"

The sky outside the plane was cloudless now. A blue so bright it hurt my eyes. My dad was touching my shoulder, but I could barely feel it.

"Tess," he said.

I looked at him and saw the concern on his face.

"Hey," he said, "where did you go?"

11

My thoughts went first to the article. The one Jonah had sent me about the Russian billionaire who wanted to upload his brain to keep from dying. At the time it hadn't seemed that important. Jonah sent me lots of articles. And videos. And GIFs. And songs. And photos. And every other piece of media you can think of.

Early on, we broke away from text alone, and for some weeks we communicated entirely in links and images. Not because we had nothing to say to each other, but because it was fun. Multimedia flirting: It kept things interesting.

But sometimes he sent articles that weren't meant to be a link in the flirt-chain. These pieces often had short accompanying messages like "Cool, right?" or "READ NOW" or just "This!" The article about the Russian had no message at all.

It just showed up in my in-box one day. I never mentioned

it to him while he was alive. I think I repressed it. But after I got the new message from his account, I went back and read it over again. And it was just as creepy as I remembered. It said that someday, there would be no difference at all between man and machine. Scientists called this concept the Singularity.

For a moment, I surrendered to complete illogic and let my mind go down that road. Maybe the Singularity had actually arrived and Jonah was still alive somewhere on the Internet. Maybe he had melded with the machine I'd used to love him. It wasn't that hard to picture.

My computer, after all, was where I'd always found him. His face, when I saw it in the rare video chat, was pixilated, sometimes freezing in a smile when my Internet connection was slow. And his g-chat messages popped up on my screen like the machine itself had generated them.

I was all set to embrace this new reality and make contact with cyber-Jonah until I took a moment to take a few deep breaths.

I was sitting at my dad's computer where I had been since we got home from the airport. I closed my eyes and listened to some birdsong coming through the window. And when I saw the new message again, I couldn't help but think of human fingers typing it.

Fingertips on keys. The same fingertips that had once—just once—rested above my hip bone. Jonah was not typing things on a keyboard anymore. He was not doing this because he had no living fingers. He had dead fingers. He was not living in a computer or in a stream of code. He was gone.

I took another long, slow breath. Then I typed my response, one letter at a time. I pressed reply and looked at the three words I had typed.

> **Who are you?**

It was the only logical question to ask. I had probably known that from the beginning. I watched the screen and waited out the two minutes it took for a response.

Not sure where to start.

I got up from my chair and walked around the room, letting my bare feet dig into the old wool rug in my father's office. Then I sat back down.

> **Start by telling me who**
> **you are . . . maybe?**

It was still Jonah's face that popped up alongside each reply, his eyes looking right at the camera, and by extension, at me.

**I'm the person you've been
talking to for the last five months.**

A real urge to shut everything down came over me.
To cancel my account. Shut off my dad's computer. Go to
sleep. Wake up in a few days. But if I did that, I might never
know anything.

**And just so I can keep from
fully going insane, that
person is not Jonah?**

This time, the response came quickly.

No.

There are TV shows about people like me. That was the
thought that bubbled up. I had watched these shows, the
ones where people think they're in love with a gorgeous
woman and it turns out to be an obese insurance manager
in the suburbs of Cleveland. But I had actually met Jonah!
I had gotten contact information directly from him.

Was I ever talking to Jonah?

A question I wasn't sure I wanted answered.

Yes.

When?

In the beginning.
The first couple months.

Then I was always
talking to you?

Yes.

The first stirrings of anger arrived then.

Has it occurred to you that
this is unspeakably fucked up?

No response.

And that you've been reading
messages I wrote for someone else.
And some I never intended anyone to
read. Private accounts of my own grief.

I couldn't stop typing.

And that you have been involved
in the cruelest kind of trick imaginable
for months of your life? Has it occurred
to you that you have done a deeply,
deeply fucked-up thing, and that you
are likely a deeply, deeply fucked-up
person?

A brief pause. Then:

Yes.

The urge to keep going was a hard one to ignore, but the one thing I knew was that I couldn't give this person anything else. So, I tried not to remember all of the things I'd said in the last month, the intimate things that I never would have spoken aloud to anyone. Things that felt safe only because I knew, deep down, they would never be read. A new message came from him:

I thought about never telling you.

Then:

**But then I actually thought
that might be worse.**

And finally:

**I never meant to keep doing it.
And I didn't know that Jonah
was going to kill himself.
I'm not sure I can really explain
it all right now. Like this.**

I stared at the screen. I was able to quell the growing rage and confusion enough to type one last line. There was only one more thing I wanted to know before I extricated myself from all of this and curled up in the fetal position on the floor. And it was something simple.

You never answered my first question.

A short pause.

My name is Daniel Torres.
I was Jonah's roommate at MIT.

A name. Of course, that was all it was. Someone else's name. I moved my cursor up to the X that would close out the page. But before I could click it, another message came through.

I'm sorry, Tess.

I pressed down on the mouse. And in an instant, all of it was gone.

12

The next week disappeared out from under me like one of those tablecloths a magician yanks clean. It was there one moment. Then it wasn't. I can only remember a few things to prove the days went by at all. First, there was the fallout from Forever Friends. Apparently, Elaine had feared the worst when I didn't turn up for evening fellowship, and within minutes, she sent people out to comb the fields to make sure I wasn't lying dead in the organic kale. This was according to my father who received an earful via voice mail.

The next day, he got a second dose once Elaine reached my mother in India. I heard him arguing with Mom for an hour, adopting the same exasperated and defeated tone I remembered from their fights in the run-up to the divorce, when suddenly he seemed never to know anything.

"How should I know?" was his catch phrase back then,

and it made its glorious return that morning. "How should I know why she came here? Why don't you ask her?" Then: "How should I know why she's dropping out of school? Do you think she tells me anything?"

Eventually he called me down to talk to her. I hadn't spoken to my mom in weeks. In the time since the divorce, she had become almost as odd and walled-off as my father, but in more socially acceptable ways.

Instead of obsessing over death, she chose life! Well, life-affirming exercise anyway. She'd always been a jogger, but once she was husband-free, she started running six miles every morning with her aggressively positive boyfriend, Lars.

Yoga came next. Everyone in her Park Slope neighborhood wore Yoga pants at all times anyway (just in case the need for Downward Dog should arise?) so it was only a matter of time before Mom caught on. Then it was love at first Cobra Pose. And these days she always seemed to be off somewhere without an Internet connection, seeking enlightenment while getting a herbal tea colonic. Or something.

I still remembered a version of her that was twenty pounds heavier and loved eating kettle corn with me on Sunday nights, laughing at bad Rom-Coms. Where had that woman gone?

"I'm in the Panchagiri Hills outside Bangalore!" she

yelled now. "Why are you choosing this moment to ruin your life?"

I had been numbly sitting in front of the TV for the last ten hours or so, and I wasn't really ready for human contact.

"Do you know Dad is burying animals now?" I asked.

I heard her sigh.

"Tessie," she said. "Please, will you tell me what you are doing?"

I imagined her in a sari, bare at the midriff, trying to pretend she wasn't from Minnesota. Did she have a bindi on her forehead? She had always been pretty. Probably the whole ashram was in love with her.

"Taking a personal health break," I told her. "I'm practicing *self-care* by not moving or speaking all day."

"What I should have done is bring you to India," she said. "What's wrong with your health?"

"Mostly it's my pesky brain," I said.

"Your brain?"

"It is filled with darkness."

More than anything, she hated when I was glib, but I refused to speak her language of enlightenment.

"You have to go back," she said. "Go back to school and see that counselor. I've been talking to her. You can still salvage the term."

"Not happening."

"Go back!" she said, as if repetition might be the key. "Go back! Go back! Go back! It's a mistake to stay with your father right now. He's not going to help you move forward. You couldn't set the bar any lower if you tried."

I didn't speak.

"I'm worried," she said in a near-whisper.

"But not worried enough to come home," I said.

"Tess," she said.

"I have to go," I said.

I handed the phone to my father. He stared at me with his hurt child look again. But I walked away and returned to my place on the couch where I proceeded to kill as many hours as I could watching the videotaped lives of B-grade celebrities. This whole situation had left me with two options as far as I could see it. 1) I could think of all the reasons why I had allowed this to happen to me, or 2) I could pretend it wasn't happening and that I wasn't actually a person. With most precincts reporting, option number two was winning in a landslide.

For the next three days I nearly absented myself from time. My father was in and out during this time, saying things to me that I barely registered, expressing concern in his detached, awkward way, sighing out of his nose, and delivering food. I went hours without remembering that he was in the house.

Until the morning of the fourth day.

I was on my fifteenth consecutive hour of reality television, and my fourth day in the same sweatpants when he walked into the living room, wearing a pressed black suit. I almost didn't recognize him at first. His midlife crisis hair was slicked back, and he looked more polished than I'd seen him in years.

"Are you going to an old person prom?" I asked, staring at the screen.

He walked right up to me and straightened his tie.

"Tessie," he said, "I'm going to need you to go upstairs and put on some real pants."

"I'm sorry," I said. "*Real* pants?"

"You know what I mean," he said. "*Pants* pants."

"Pants pants," I mouthed to myself.

He grabbed the remote and turned off the television.

"And a nice shirt. Black if you have it."

"I don't," I said.

But he was already walking out of the room. I had the shades pulled, and without the light from the television, the room was completely dark.

"What the hell is going on?" I asked.

"I'll wait for you in the car," he said. "We're going to a funeral."

An hour later, I was wearing the realest pants I had, standing in the parking lot of Honey Creek Nature Preserve. I didn't see a creek. Or any honey. But all around us were beautiful trees. Towering jack pines with gray-green needles and a few pale blue spruces—the names came back to me from Girl Scout Camp. I saw no sign of a funeral, though.

"Now what?" I asked.

"Now," said my father, "we hike."

He set off walking ahead of me, and I followed a few steps behind.

In the car on the way over, he had pretended like nothing had happened in the last few days. He didn't mention my brooding, or ask me what was going on, and for once, I was thankful for his self-absorption. Instead of prying, he briefed me on *his* situation. Essentially, he had been double-crossed. He was hired to do a funeral for someone named Maxine Harp, and now the client's family had pulled out without ever telling him.

"Do you know what a pre-need deal is?" he asked me.

I shook my head.

"Basically, you meet with someone before they die and

lock in costs for their funeral. The price of funeral real estate is always rising, so if you want to be buried, buying a plot early is a good idea. You can prepay for embalming liquid, mortician's services, and even your burial gown. It's a good way to get business ahead of time."

"So, you had a pre-need deal with Maxine?" I asked.

He nodded.

"But you don't have the money?"

He avoided my stare.

"They used an insurance company as a buffer. They have the money. We had an unspoken agreement."

His voice was soft when he said this. It was clear he felt now like an unspoken ass.

"So, what kind of animal is Maxine. A lemur?" I asked.

"What?" said my dad. "She's a human!"

"Oh," I said. "Huh."

"What's that supposed to mean?"

"Nothing. I'm just surprised that an actual person wanted you to do a funeral. Did you get her wasted or something?"

My father tightened his grip on the wheel. His face was starting to redden. I tried to backtrack.

"I mean, I'm sure it's similar to doing animals, right. Just like . . . less hairy."

"Please stop talking," said Dad.

I was surprised by the fragile tone of his voice.

"Dad," I said.

"Enough," he said.

A bug spattered against the windshield. Dad turned on the wipers, but all it did was smear a streak across the glass. He looked straight ahead.

"You think I want to bury pets for the rest of my life?" he said. "I just kind of fell into that when nothing else was happening. Give me a little credit, Tess."

He sighed.

"This was supposed to be my first big break."

We were walking down the trailhead now into some dense woods. The obituary in the paper said that both Maxine's burial and service would take place here, but still, we saw no evidence of mourners. There were no markers or headstones along the path. No music in the air. Still we kept trudging forward, listening to the whirring of insects and the watery chirps of darting swallows. I watched my father's disconsolate march, and somewhere in my frosty, shattered heart I felt a small pang of something.

"What were you going to do?" I asked.

"For the funeral?"

I nodded.

"If you're just going to make fun of me," he said, "I'd rather not discuss it."

We tromped onward.

"I'm genuinely curious," I said. "You're famous for doing this crazy stuff, right? So lay it on me. What was your plan for Maxine the human?"

I could tell he was still pissed at me, but he smiled in spite of himself.

"It was going to be a marathon."

He was quiet for a moment, but when he started talking again, it was in a fast, excited voice.

"Maxine Harp was a ninety-year-old runner. She started at the age of seventy, and kept at it. Each year she ran the New York Marathon and then she was interviewed by the *Today Show*. She always said she wanted to die in her running shoes. So, her service was going to be an honorary run."

His eyes widened.

"I'm talking torches. Engraved medals. T-shirts. Starting pistols. And chauffeurs for people who wanted to watch from a limo. Then, at the end: another marathon. Of food this time. All her favorites to replace the calories burned in her honor! It was going to be epic! A trek to honor her life's journey in the . . ."

He tripped suddenly and went stumbling shoulder-first into the dirt of the trail.

"Ow," he said. "Dammit."

"Whoa, Dad. Are you okay?"

He got up, wincing. The entire left side of his suit was wet and dirty. He tried his best to dust himself clean.

"What happened?" I asked.

Instead of answering, he just knelt down and pushed aside some brush from the side of the trail. Underneath it was a cream-colored stone with something engraved on it. I knelt beside him. It read, Ella Olson, 1965–2012. A gravestone. Beneath Ella's name it read: "From my rotting body, flowers shall grow and I am in them and that is eternity."

"Edvard Munch," I said right away.

My dad looked at me, surprised.

"I studied him in art class."

He got up and started walking again.

"I guess this is a cemetery after all," he said.

Now that we were looking down, we spotted stones in other places. They were flat and unobtrusive, scattered here and there like the last remains of an old civilization.

"Hey," I said. "I'm sorry."

My dad broke his stare at the ground.

"For what?" he said, his voice a little shaky.

"Your funeral. It sounded cool. I'm sure it would have been great."

He took a long breath and then nodded.

"Thanks," he said.

And as we made our way through the grass, and over a small dribbling creek, we eventually caught the sound of a voice coming from the top of a hill. When we looked up, there were a few wisps of white smoke in the air. We could just make out a sparse crowd, their heads all cocked in the same direction. My dad looked at me with a "what now?" kind of glance.

"Now we hike," I said.

13

No one was dressed in black.

That's what I noticed first. Instead the mourners wore earth tones. Loose khaki pants. Gortex hiking boots. Like they were on a death safari or something. And they were all gathered around a simple hole in the ground.

The dirt was piled to the side, and surrounding the opening there were wildflowers scattered in a loose border. Just to the right of the grave was a body wrapped in a bright white shroud. Maxine was small and tied up like a birthday present with more flowers under one of the lowering straps.

We made our way to the back of the crowd. No one paid us much notice. The service was coming to an end. A man in a tweed coat burned sage while an older woman in a billowy cotton dress spoke in a lilting voice.

". . . although she has created a *rupture* in our lives, she is nourishing the trees and the grasses and the flowers the way she nourished her family. And just as she preserved the optimism of so many women of advanced age, she will now preserve wildlife with the nutrients of her body."

Two younger guys walked over to the body.

"Her sons," my dad whispered to me.

They lifted their mother's shroud over the grave's opening. She hovered beneath their strained wrists like she was levitating.

"Earth to earth," began the woman in the robe. "Ashes to ashes."

Hand-over-hand, a foot at a time, the boys slowly lowered the shroud-enclosed body into the ground until Maxine Harp disappeared.

"Dust to dust."

Nobody moved. Except one of the Harp boys, who walked solemnly over to the pile of dirt and unearthed a digging shovel. He stuck it into the small hill and pulled up a shovelful. Then he carried it back to the grave, and let the soil tumble back into the place where it came from.

He wasn't crying, but it looked like he might start any minute. His brother came up behind him and took the shovel from his hands. He, too, walked to the pile, scooped and unloaded his dirt. A sister came next, and one by one, all Maxine's children and grandchildren took turns filling in the grave. When the last shovelful of dirt hit home, my dad turned away from the ceremony and began to walk away.

"Where are you going?" I asked. "Don't you want to talk to these guys?"

He picked up his pace.

"We're not supposed to be here," he said.

"What do you mean?" I said. "These people screwed you over."

He shook his head.

"I was hired to do a job," he said. "And then I was fired. This is a service industry. We're not here for the right reasons."

We were almost back over the hill when a voice came from behind us.

"Duncan," it said. "Is that you?"

It was one of the Harp boys, jogging toward us, his large hand reaching out like he was flagging a cab.

"I thought it was you," he said.

"Yeah," said my dad, "I just . . ."

"It was big of you to come," said the large guy. Up close, he looked like a giant, though he was probably only an inch or two taller than my dad.

"That was a lovely ceremony," my dad said.

And I was surprised to hear his voice give out at the end. The Harp boy clapped a hand down on my dad's shoulder.

"I wanted to invite you," he said, "but my brother said we shouldn't since we . . . went in another direction."

He looked down and his grin fell away.

"Look, Duncan, I'm not going to tell you that the news about your deal in Nantucket didn't have an effect on our decision. But, Mom loved the outdoors. And then she met this woman with a green burial company, who told her about this place. No coffins. No embalming. No chemicals. Just nature and stuff. Mom changed everything at the last minute. This was what she wanted."

"I see," said Dad.

"That's her by the way," said the giant, squinting into the sun. "The gal in the beige."

I looked up toward the grave and felt something in me drop.

"That's . . . who?" I asked.

He looked down at me, startled. I'm not sure he had even seen me until now.

"The lady with the company. Greener Pastures. That's her."

"Greener Pastures," I said.

She was waving to us now, the woman in beige. Her light

blond hair was pulled up into a clip, loose strands spilling down her neck. Her nose and forehead, even at this distance, were darkened with freckles and flushed from the sun.

"Her name's Grace," he said. "Would you like to meet her?"

I looked at my dad. He looked back at me. We started walking straight toward her. At the last minute, she caught sight of us and smiled.

"Duncan," she said. "Tess! I wondered if I might see you again. Welcome to Maxine's planting."

Grace the Traitor.

This time she was wearing a tunic dress over tights, with a shawl draped across her shoulders. No makeup. In her earth tones, she looked like a forest nymph. A traitorous forest nymph.

"Planting?" I said.

"That's what we call them, Tess."

"Is her body going to grow into a field of corn?"

Grace looked around to see if anyone was in earshot.

"You're upset about something."

My dad stared at the ground.

"You're right," I said. "We're just a teensy bit upset about the fact that you poached a goddamn funeral from us, Grace. You double-crossing hippie!"

"I didn't even know you were in the business," my dad said, more to himself than to her.

Grace looked at me for a minute. Her voice shifted to a stressed whisper.

"I didn't *poach* anything. I met a family that needed my services, and I happily provided them. I assume that's a lot like what your dad does."

I took a step toward Grace.

"And I'm sure you had no idea that someone else had already agreed to *plant* Ms. Harp."

Grace adjusted her shawl and swept a lock of hair away from her eyes.

"They might have mentioned something. . . ."

The crowd was dispersing around us, friends and family members tromping over the preserve, pointing out the pastoral beauty to one another.

"I've met enough liars lately," I said, "to know when I'm looking at one."

I grabbed my dad's arm.

"C'mon, Dad," I said. "Grace, enjoy your planting. I hope the harvest is bountiful."

I managed to yank him forward, and we started to walk away.

"Hold on," said Grace. "Wait a second. Will you, Tess?"

I don't know why I turned back, but when I did, she looked chastened.

"What?" I said. "What is it?"

Her lips were slightly pursed.

"How are you doing?" she asked.

My hands flexed in my pockets. I thought about my last week, the way I had been duped and crushed over and over again.

"I've been watching a lot of television," I said. "Thanks for asking."

Grace fiddled with a button on her dress.

"Duncan," she said, "can you give us a minute?"

My dad didn't protest. He turned around and looked out over the preserve, taking it all in.

"Have you told your father yet?" Grace asked.

"Told him what?"

"How bad things really were that day?"

"How bad were they?" I asked.

"I don't know," said Grace. "Only you can answer that. . . ."

I looked at her face, and beneath the tan and the freckles, there were rings under her eyes.

". . . but it seemed pretty bad."

"Really? And what would you know about it?" I asked. "Are you a high school guidance counselor? Have you read some really good self-help books that you want to recommend to me?"

"No," said Grace. "Nothing like that."

For a moment it seemed like this was maybe going to be the end of our conversation. Then she spoke again.

"But I have been so depressed that I didn't leave my house for a month. So there's that. And I've ruined a marriage because of my own personal misery. And I've thought of doing things much more irrational than jumping off a dock. It's okay if you don't want to hear this from me. I get it. But the reason I know about you, Tess, is that I've *been* you."

I wanted to yell at her, to flip her off and leave. But I was rooted in place.

"I'm sorry I lied," she said. "I didn't know your father was the competition. If you ever want to talk to me when you're not so angry, you can contact me here."

She handed me a card, and I held it between my thumb and forefinger. My instinct was to drop it on the ground, let it biodegrade the way it was probably meant to. But, I didn't do that. Instead, I slipped it into the pocket of my real pants, and then I walked back to the car and drove home with my sulking father.

14

I saw this news story a couple years ago about a guy who loved someone for ten years and then discovered she didn't exist. For an entire decade he thought he was dating a fitness model in LA, this spandex-clad girl next door with a blond ponytail and perky boobs. In reality, he was being duped by a bored housewife in West Virginia. His true love was just a digital collage of images from posters and videos, fused into a Facebook Frankenstein's monster.

In the news segment I watched, they showed all his e-mails: thousands of pages piled on his desk like the longest romance novel ever written. There were boxes, too, stacked crates of gifts, photos, and tokens from their relationship. He even had a tattoo of her face on his right shoulder.

I still remember the look on his face when the reporter asked him how he could have possibly fallen for the scam. How could he really *not have known* it was a hoax all that time? Ten years! His face had turned red at first, but then he looked defiant, his wet eyes full of life.

"I was in love," he said.

And what could the reporter really say after that?

I understand that look now.

Since my contact with Daniel the fake, I'd pretty much felt all of the feelings there are to feel. Rage and self-pity? Check. Astonishment with a hint of denial? Check. Short bouts of hopelessness ending with the occasional manic laughing fit? Yep.

There was so much that I had to rethink. So many moments that weren't what I thought they were. It felt like I was living them all over again. Memories came back and I had to completely reevaluate them.

The video of the starlings, for instance. Even something small like that. Just a snippet of footage with tiny black birds flying in pulsing patterns over a pastel sky. A "murmuration" it's called. Along with this video file, there was accompanying text.

This is what my body feels like when I think about you.

Who sent it? It had arrived in my in-box right around the three-month mark.

No-man's-land.

But it's important because I responded, at the time, by sending the first naked picture of myself I'd ever taken. I know. I get it. Spare me your judgments. It just seemed right at the time. I let my dress fall to the floor along with my tights, bra, and underwear, and I snapped the picture by holding a phone to the mirror on my closet door.

I made no attempt to hide the stuff about my body I hate. My outie belly button. The constellation of moles on my right thigh. A half-moon scar over my hip from a bicycle accident. My noticeably uneven breasts. I wrote back:

> **This is what my body looks like when you think about it.**

I knew I shouldn't be sending it even as I did it. I'd heard all the warnings. But what no one ever tells you is that the risk itself is the point; it's the thrill of making a mistake on purpose. The only problem is that I thought I was making that mistake for someone in particular. Someone I knew.

Honestly, though, the sex stuff didn't bother me as much as I thought. Worse were the things I told him. Stuff I hadn't told anyone else. The way I used to shoot baskets in my parents' driveway in junior high, telling myself that if

I could just hit ten free throws in a row, I would no longer be ugly. My fear of the dark, all the way into high school, and the way I used to leave my blinds open so I could see the light from the neighbors' TV.

The time I got my first period at a pool party and had to call my mom to bring me home. The time I watched all my friends make fun of an overweight girl in gym class until they brought her to tears, and I did nothing to stop them. And the admission, absolutely true, that I'd never had a boyfriend until him.

Some of these things made it to Jonah, I know. We spoke on the phone occasionally at first, and I remember his low voice saying "it's okay," and "but you were just a kid." He hardly ever returned the favor, though. He wasn't good at revealing. The only time I can remember clearly was when he told me about being hospitalized for a weekend when he was sixteen.

"All I can tell you, Tess, is that I felt worse than I ever had in my life. And I wasn't sure what I was going to do if I was left alone. My mom found me staring into the knife drawer in the kitchen, and when she asked me why, I couldn't answer. She called my doctor and he helped make the arrangements at a place nearby."

I asked him if he'd ever felt that way again.

"No," he said. "But I have to take a pill every day. Probably for the rest of my life."

It might have been the last real thing I found out about him. Soon after that, he wasn't interested in the phone as much. He wanted to text and chat, claiming he felt "more like himself" that way. And who was I to deny him? I liked the way he sounded in writing. I imagined us as a famous intellectual couple from history, exchanging "correspondence." I had still never read anything as sexy and strange as Flaubert's letter to Louise Colet in 1846.

Mr. Barthold had mentioned something about these letters when we were reading *Madame Bovary* for A.P. Lit, and I had quickly looked them up. What I found was better than I could have imagined.

"I will cover you with love when next I see you, with caresses, with ecstasy. I want to gorge you with all the joys of the flesh, so that you faint and die . . . when you are old, I want you to recall those few hours, I want your dry bones to quiver with joy when you think of them."

Damn, Gustave!

I wanted to be written to in that way, and Jonah came close.

Daniel, I suppose, came close, too.

I stayed away from Facebook for a week after that first

exchange with Daniel. When I finally logged back on, I found a single message sitting in my in-box. It was not from Jonah's account this time. It was from someone that I wasn't friends with. The profile picture was not a face. It was a white silhouette with a light blue background, a template for a future image.

The message read:

Hello, Tess.
First of all, I don't expect you to get in touch with me again.

This isn't a plea for that to happen. I just wanted to explain some things to you in case you are curious about them in the future. Then, I promise I won't contact you again.

Here goes.

First: I believe Jonah stopped communicating with you because he didn't want you to know what was going wrong with him, psychologically. He didn't want anyone to know much about that. I didn't fully understand this at the time, but now I'm sure about it.

Second: I started using his account because I wanted him

to break up with you the right way instead of just shutting down. That was my plan. To break up with you as him in a gentle way. I know this doesn't really make sense, but at the time I thought it did.

Third: Once we started writing to each other, I was not able to break up with you. Either as him or as me.

That's all.

I'm not sure what I expect you to do with this information. I just wanted you to have it. You have plenty of reasons to distrust me, but I still feel the need to tell you that I have never done anything like this before. And I'm not quite sure how it all happened. I do know that I have made a terrible situation much worse and I hope you can forgive me someday.

Okay,
Daniel.

P.S. I think Jonah would have been in love with you if he was capable of being in love with anyone. But I'm not sure he was when you met him.

I read the message twice. The first time my eyes skated over the sentences, not really taking them in. The second time, I read them carefully. I looked at the white space where Daniel's photo should be, the face-mold sitting empty. I wanted to cry, but I couldn't. I didn't know if any of it was true.

The smartest thing to do, I thought, might be to accept these sentences as possibilities and leave it at that. I could take Daniel at his word and never contact him again. But there was this damn word stuck in my head. The woman at Maxine's funeral had used it and I kept hearing it over and over.

"Rupture."

It was the closest anyone had come to describing how I felt when I learned of Jonah's death. Something inside me had burst apart suddenly, and I was still willing to try anything I could to put it back together.

So far, things had only grown more confusing, but if there was even a small chance that some of the pieces could snap back into place again, didn't I have to try to make that happen? An idea came to me, and the fact that I was a little scared by it, made me think it might be the right one.

I quickly typed a message. It was short, but there was no chance of misinterpreting it. I watched it sitting there in the text box, the cursor blinking at the end of the final line. Then I hit Reply and let out a deep breath.

It read:

No more computers.
612-555-0491

15

I canceled my Facebook account later that day.

I went to the Delete Account page, entered my password, and when asked if I was sure I would like to permanently delete my account, I clicked yes. I cleared my history. I did not back up my data. All my preferences disappeared along with the version of myself that I had so carefully made.

I killed the things that defined me. Every band. Every movie. Every witty quote. Every video. Every flattering photo. Gone. I deleted Jonah's girlfriend. I was still that person in a server somewhere, but other than that, I had disappeared. When I was done with all this I felt a little better.

Then I went to the bathroom and threw up.

Instead of looking into the toilet, I closed my eyes and tried to remember all the things from Jonah/Daniel that I had just erased. I flipped through them in my head. Song playlists, including one that just looped "Thirteen" by Big

Star over and over because it was "the purest love song ever written, seriously."

Other playlists disappeared too, including: WEEN + THE BEATLES = TRUE LOVE, SONGS MY GRANDPARENTS PROBABLY HAD SEX TO, SONGS WITH QUESTION-ABLE METAPHORS, and IF YOU DON'T CRY WHEN YOU HEAR THIS THEN YOU ARE A COLD COLD HUMAN WITH AN ICY ICY HEART.

I lost the links to the videos, too. The Starlings. The supercut of Bollywood dance scenes. Sloth and Chunk from *The Goonies*. A Ted Talk about the neuroscience of love. And a barrage of strange homemade happy birthday videos scavenged from the junk heap of YouTube.

The messages were gone, too. All 788 of them to be exact.

Some of them were just a line or two. Others the equivalent of twenty typed pages. Late night manifestos full of bad jokes and melodramatic vows. Some of them from Jonah. Some of them . . . not. I could remember a few phrases from early on.

Just write me two more words and I'll be happy forever.

This was never supposed to happen to me, didn't anyone ever tell you that?

You have me in a wild way, Tess Fowler.

And always an allusion to seeing me "soon."

Soon was always coming. How soon? *So* soon. When school was over. Over Spring break. Summer break, for sure. "We'll work in the same place. It's going to happen *soon*." But soon never showed, and eventually even the assurances ran out.

His messages went next.

For two entire days there was no communication. No videos. No songs. No links. No chats. I wrote. I called. I got nothing in return. Then eventually, Jonah's wall came alive with messages again. But not the kind I wanted to see.

At first, I couldn't believe they were real. They had to be a joke. The worst joke in history. "Sweet, Jonah, I had no idea your soul was hurting so much." "I will never under-stand this. Never." "Come back. I miss you already."

I contacted MIT and was passed from administrator to administrator until I screamed into the phone at a woman who sounded like a friendly grandmother.

"Just tell me if he's really dead," I said. "Please!"

And the woman said, "Yes, honey. He is. I'm so very sorry."

And then I hung up and walked away from Quaker school without a coat on a cool early spring morning in Iowa. It had been weeks since the last frost, and the corn was just beginning to come up in the fields around me. I walked along the highway, following a line of barbed wire as it sliced across the pegs of a wooden fence.

There were tire ruts in the shoulder of the highway from ATVs, and I walked in their grooves. I walked for hours, blinking away hot tears and wiping my nose with my shirt-sleeve. My only nice pair of boots soaked up the wet mud. Eventually I came across a sign for Model Train Land, a hokey roadside stop a few miles in the distance.

I first saw the signs when my dad drove me to Quaker school in the fall. We'd joked about stopping, about it being a cultural embassy for my new state. THE LARGEST MODEL TRAIN RAILROAD EVER BUILT! ONLY 2 MILES! YOU'RE JUST 1 MILE AWAY FROM MODEL TRAIN LAND! ALL ABOARD!

I walked until I reached it: the smallest museum in the world. It was just a ranch house, painted red, fifty feet from the freeway. The place was open, but it was a week-day, so it was empty when I stepped inside. I scraped together the entrance fee from a wad of small bills and coins in my pocket and I paid a red-nosed old man in a striped conductor's hat. He smiled a gummy smile and handed me a wooden whistle. Then I stepped inside the cramped space and stood in front of the glass enclosed train world.

The track was bright silver and it crisscrossed an elaborate diorama of scenery from all over the country. Snowcapped mountains. A calm ocean. Winding rivers banked by flowering trees, their leaves made from green toothbrush bristles. There were old-fashioned telephone poles and farm windmills with tiny spinning blades. The trains zipped in and out of tunnels, making their way over the entirety of their circular world again and again.

At first I was soothed by it. Everything was so carefully placed; there was nothing disorderly about this toy universe. The small homes next to the rows of shops on Main Street reminded me of places I'd stopped on the way to visit grandparents when I was a girl. Places I'd imagine living in for the time it took to drink a creamy milk shake at an old-fashioned soda fountain.

Train Land was a peaceful, easy land. But, the longer I stayed there, the less comforted I felt. Something about it was bothering me. It took me another minute or two to realize what it was. Although, it was a flawless place, there were no people in it.

It was emptied of souls.

I got up from my knees in the bathroom now and flushed the toilet. I splashed handfuls of cool water on my face, and swished some mouthwash that made my gums burn.

I heard my father coming up the stairs behind me, and as I wiped off my face with a towel, I was already trying to look normal again. I took a few deep breaths. And when he knocked on the bathroom door, I opened it with a look on my face that I hoped betrayed nothing. He stepped back from the door, his hands in his pockets. Then he cleared his throat and looked me in the eyes.

"I made some dinner," he said. "And I want to talk to you about something."

16

It was true. My dad actually cooked dinner that night.

It felt like the first time in years. Back when my parents were still together, he was head chef of the household. He'd spend his idle mornings (which was most of them) at the farmers' market downtown, picking out the perfect deep purple eggplants for his parmigiana. After the divorce, though, it was all Lean Cuisines and Lean Pockets. If it didn't have Lean in the title, he wouldn't eat it. Yet, he was still a couple pounds overweight. Go figure.

Tonight, he made a roast chicken with potatoes. It was simple, but after a week and a half of takeout, it tasted like a revelation. We ate in silence for a while before he set his fork down, brushed the hair away from his face, and rested his hands on the table.

"I know what you're thinking," he said.

For a second, I thought he really did.

"What?" I said.

"I know you're thinking this funeral planning business is just another bad idea of mine. I have a track record. I understand that. And some of my other . . . projects haven't exactly worked out, at least by conventional standards. But, I want you to understand. This one is different."

I stabbed a potato and avoided eye contact. I should have known that dinner wasn't going to be free. It came with a lecture. When he spoke again, the tone of his voice had shifted.

"Do you remember when Grandma died?" he asked.

"Of course," I said.

My dad's mom had died two years ago of a rare degenerative lung disease, and Dad spent most of the last days with her in hospice. I visited a couple times, but the place was too sad. By the end, we just sat in silence, listening to the hiss of her breathing machine.

"I let your aunt Ruby handle most of the arrangements for the funeral," he said. "I don't know why I did that. I was unnerved, I guess. All the coffins sounded like luxury cars, and every step of the way people were trying to upsell me. I couldn't make all those decisions while I was grieving. It was too much."

He took a sip of water.

"But I knew everything was wrong when we showed up

to that huge church for her funeral. Remember that place? It was like the Taj Mahal. And they put that fancy purple cloth over her coffin. Grandma was never very religious. In the hospice she told me to stop the priest from coming around. She said he looked like 'death in a nightgown.' Then, at her funeral, she got a priest whether she wanted one or not."

"He was awful," I said.

"And that service was so self-righteous and boring! My mom wasn't like that. I heard most of my dirty jokes from her. She liked to sing in the car, remember? That old Chrysler? And she loved those kids at the school cafeteria where she worked. She had life! That place. The tone. None of it was right."

His eyes were widening now.

"And so I started thinking that day. Why do funerals have to be this way? Where is the real sense of the person you knew? Where is the joy along with the sadness? Would it kill someone to make a joke? The worst has already happened, right? I couldn't stop worrying over these problems. I was obsessed. And I wanted to make a change."

"So you started cremating dogs?"

"I started making coffins," he said. "A week later. People thought I had lost my mind. Your mom was gone by then, but even she was concerned. And maybe she should have been. But the first thing I made when I knew what I was doing was a replacement coffin for Grandma."

"Holy crap. You dug her up?"

He sighed.

"Just listen, will you? I worked on the thing for months. She kept a postcard of Monet's poplar trees near her bed at the hospice, so the wood was an easy choice. I sanded that poplar until it was smooth as sea glass. I finished it off with bronze handles, and an intricate woven pattern on top. Finally, I carved her name on the lid."

"Joy," I said.

"Joy," he said, and smiled. "It was too late to give it to her obviously. So, I went to her house and I filled the casket with her stuff. Some of it, anyway. The old FM radio she used for listening to baseball games. Some photos of her as a girl, tan and smiling on a dock in Northern Minnesota. That sparkly green sequined sweater she wore. Then I dug a second grave in her backyard and I laid it to rest there. It's like a time capsule now, I guess."

"Whoa," I said. "You buried it back there?"

"It took me all afternoon."

"That's actually pretty great," I said.

"Yeah," he said. "But it still didn't seem like enough. People need to rethink all of this stuff. We need a new culture around death. And why can't I be the one to help start it? Somebody has to. Maybe this is what I'm supposed to do."

He got up and walked over to the fridge. He pulled out a can of beer and cracked it open. Then he looked at me.

"Maybe it's what *we* are supposed to do."

I returned to my food. I took a bite of chicken and chewed it slowly.

"We?" I said.

"Haven't you been thinking about it? Since Florida?"

I stuffed more food in my mouth.

"I don't know," I lied. "Not really."

He took a sip of beer.

"Well, I've thought it all out. I'll pay you. We'll work out the percentage. If you're not going to go to school for a while, you need a job."

My dad had never been a great disciplinarian, and his stern glance looked like an empty threat. He quickly switched tactics.

"Look. I want this business to work," he said, "and I've realized I can't do it by myself. I don't have all the skills I need. I could use you, Tess. You showed me something in Ocala. You understand people. You know what they want. I think you might have a knack for this."

I watched him carefully. A lock of graying hair hung over

his right eye. He didn't brush it away. I wished I could trust him entirely, that I could feel nothing but good about all of this. But it was too easy to remember other promises he'd made. The way he had changed in the last few years. Just because he was acting more like his old self tonight, didn't mean all was forgotten.

"What kind of partnership are we talking about?" I asked. "Do I actually get a say in things?"

"Sure," he said. "That's the point. I want you to weigh in."

He fidgeted at the table. I stopped to think. It had been a while since I'd had any leverage in a situation.

"I have two conditions," I said.

He narrowed his eyes.

"Okay . . ."

"First, any extra profits we make go back in my college account."

My dad pursed his lips.

"You just dropped out of high school," he said. "Why do you need a college account?"

I looked down at my plate.

"It's the principle," I said. "That money was mine, and you spent it like an a-hole. Either you agree to repay it, or there's no deal."

He wiped some condensation off the table with his palm.

"Fine," he said. "I told you I'd pay you back. See. Now I'm going to. Are we good?"

"No," I said. "We're not."

"What else?"

"Condition two: I'm not going back to Forever Friends," I said. "And you have to defend me when Mom tries to make me. I'm done there. No more community building. No more farming. The Quakers are fine, but I'm not one of them."

"I'll do my best," he said.

"Your best isn't good enough," I said. "I actually want results."

"Done," he said.

"Condition three: Hand me your beer," I said.

"You said there were two conditions."

"I lied."

He squinted at me.

"You're not taking this beer," he said.

I waited, expressionless.

It took him a second, but gradually he slid the can down my way. I grabbed it and filled half my empty water glass. Then I slid it back to him.

"I'm not toasting you with water," I said, and held up my glass.

He held up his half-empty beer can.

"Morituri te salutant," I said.

He lowered the can.

"What does that mean?"

"It's Latin. It means 'those who are about to die, salute you!' Criminals used to say it before dying for Caesar in staged naval battles. It seems appropriate now that we're making a living on corpses. Don't you think?"

My father considered this a moment.

"Okay," he said. *"Morituri te salutant."*

We air-toasted. Then we drank.

And that's how I became a funeral planner.

17

The first phone call came that same night.

I heard the sound coming from upstairs: a muffled chime echoing through the hallway. It got louder at the foot of the stairs. I went up to the guest room and found my cell phone ringing on the dresser. I thought I had turned it off. I didn't remember switching it back on. I looked down at the unfamiliar number. I pressed talk.

There was silence on the line. Then a soft, unsure voice.

"Is this . . . Tess?"

It was not a low voice like Jonah's, but somehow I recognized it without having heard it before. I looked down at the screen again, at the seconds of the call ticking away. Slowly, I brought the phone back to my ear. Then I sat down on the bed, took a breath, and said: "That depends. Who wants to know?"

More silence.

"I didn't think this would actually be your number," he said.

"Why would I give you a fake one?"

This signaled another long pause.

"I don't know," he said. "I guess you wouldn't."

Each time Daniel Torres spoke, I was surprised to hear his voice. I was surprised that it existed at all.

"I'm sorry," I said after a while. "Is this weird for you or something?"

No response.

"I mean, is it strange to talk to another human being without an element of deep deception in the mix? I can't imagine how tough this must be for you."

I had told myself to stay calm—not to get too upset before I had the chance to learn something—but it was difficult.

"Maybe . . . this isn't a good idea," he said finally.

I was lying down on my bed, the taste of stale beer on my tongue. The ceiling above my bed was cracked and peeling.

"Christ," I said. "Of course it isn't a good idea. How could it be? I don't know you. You're nothing but a creepy stranger to me. I don't even know where you're calling from."

"Romeoville," he said right away.

His voice was a little louder this time.

"Where?" I said.

"Romeoville, Illinois," he said. "It's a suburb of Chicago. By Joliet."

This time it was my turn to pause.

"Romeoville by Joliet?" I said, "That sounds totally made up."

"It isn't," he said. "It's totally real. I'm looking at it right now. It's as boring as ever."

"And that's where you grew up?"

"No. We moved around a lot. My dad's a flight instructor."

For some reason, this seemed like the oddest thing in the world to me. The father of this person I had known but not known taught people to fly airplanes in Illinois.

"So," he said. "What else?"

Still stuck in thought, I barely heard his question.

"What's that?" I said.

"What else do you want to know about me? So I'm less of a creepy stranger. If that's . . . you know . . . possible."

Honestly, I wasn't sure what I wanted to know about him. Maybe I just wanted to know he was a real person, to hear a voice. But he had opened the door, so I started asking questions. One after the next. And this is what I learned:

Daniel was an only child like me. His dad was Mexican American and his mom was white. He grew up speaking two languages, but he mostly hung out with white kids in his suburban high school and he didn't have much of an opportunity to use his Spanish.

What else?

He was eighteen years old.

What else?

His parents were still together, but they seemed to get along only when he was around as a buffer. He hardly ever saw them talking alone.

What else?

He wasn't sure what color his eyes were; his driver's license said hazel. His mom thought they were brown.

What else?

His first job was working the drive-through window at Dairy Queen. Most people spoke too loud into the microphone making his ears ring. And the bags of soft serve mix looked like digestive fluids.

What else?

The first person to die in his life was his cousin who drowned while swimming in a river with a strong current.

What else?

He was bullied in high school for being dorky and really into computer games.

What else?

His favorite place was the Natural History Museum in Chicago.

What else?

His favorite holiday was the Fourth of July because he used to be a bit of a pyro.

What else?

He didn't know his favorite color because, okay, he was color blind.

What else?

He really did play video games too much.

What else?

He didn't know why he couldn't break up with me as Jonah, or why he had kept doing what he did. He was still confused about it all and maybe that was why it was kind of hard to talk to me.

"Okay, sure," I said, breaking off our game of twenty questions, "But I want to know what your endgame was. Did you ever once think of that when you were lying to me for half a year?"

I could feel my face getting hot. I was holding my breath tight in my chest.

"I don't know."

He was tentative suddenly.

"Yes, you do!" I said. "Even if you didn't think about it consciously, you had to have some kind of idea in the back of your mind. Some sort of fantasy about what would happen."

"I guess I thought—"

"No more lies," I said softly. "If you ever want to talk to me again, which probably isn't going to happen anyway, you have to tell the truth."

He took a medium-size pause. Then he said: "I thought I would tell you and then you would love me."

"That's it? That's what you thought?"

"Yes. You would love me or I would end it as Jonah and you would never know."

"And you would have manipulated me for months without telling me. End of story."

"Yes."

"Why did you think that was okay?"

"I didn't."

"Did Jonah ever know?"

"At first. But he stopped going online after awhile."

"Wait a minute. He knew what you were doing and he didn't care?"

Daniel took a shallow breath.

"He didn't care."

It was perfectly clear to me then: I had reached my limit.

"I can't talk anymore today," I said.

"Tess."

"No more. Stop saying things."

Ten seconds of dead air. Then Daniel spoke again in his soft voice.

"Listen, I have to ask you a question, though. Just one."

I didn't answer.

"You could never tell the difference between me and Jonah? You never sensed anything? The whole time?"

I thought of that poor sad man from the TV show. The guy who'd been duped. I closed my eyes.

"I can't talk anymore today," I said again.

This time I meant it. And I ended the call.

I didn't move from the bed when I hung up. I stayed where I was for at least fifteen minutes, the back of my head pinned to the headboard. I was thinking of a moment, one that popped into my mind while I was talking to Daniel.

It was the aftermath of another high school party. One where I had basically been drinking alone in the company of others again—a pattern I'd done little to change since the farmhouse.

I wasn't drunk, though, when I came home from the party. Just a little buzzed and frustrated. While I was out, Emma had given herself a haircut in the sink. Her blond locks were scattered all over my toothbrush, in my makeup, in a trail across the floor. Outside my window, there was a group of drunk boys tackling one another in the courtyard, calling out homophobic names. I sat down at my computer and dashed off a message.

> I'm dropping out. I'm
> coming to live with you.
> Get ready.

He always seemed to be close to some device, and it never took long to get a response. This time was no exception.

You don't even know me.

It was odd, looking back. We usually indulged each other's fantasies with few exceptions. At the time I thought he meant that we hadn't seen each other enough in person, which was undoubtedly true.

Now, I knew it must have been Daniel. And he was exactly right.

> **That's what the
> honeymoon is for . . .**

At the time, I shut off my computer and went to bed. And the next day, he sent an audio file of *Chapel of Love* and we carried on as usual. Now I couldn't help wondering what might have happened if I'd asked him to explain himself that night. *How* didn't I know him?

If I had pressed him, would he have told me everything I didn't know?

18

Grace's business card was thick and grainy to the touch.

I had been holding it for the last ten minutes, looking at every detail and trying to decide if I should call her. The card had a small picture of a bright green tree filled with birds on it. Adorable. Next to the tree were the words "Greener Pastures," and then the name "Grace Ware," along with her contact information. On the back, in the lower left corner, it said, "Made with soy and vegetable inks. Chemical-free processing."

"Oh, thank God. Vegetable inks," I said to no one.

Then I dialed the number and held my breath.

"Grace with Greener Pastures," she answered right away.

Her voice left me momentarily stunned.

"Um . . ."

"Are you trying to reach Greener Pastures, miss?"

"Not yet I hope," I said.

"Tess, is that you?"

I bit my bottom lip.

"Tess?"

"What?"

"Are you there?"

"Maybe."

I heard her exhale into the phone.

"Why are you calling, Tess?"

"You told me to."

"I told you to call if you weren't angry."

I was sitting in the passenger seat of my dad's car. He was in the grocery store, buying food for the week. I had been thinking about Jonah and Daniel, trying not to succumb to the dread when I reached into my pants pocket and her card was there.

"How do you do it?" I asked.

I looked out the windshield at the people going in and out of the store, stubbing out cigarettes, dragging their kids along. I suddenly wanted to cry for the futility of the world.

"Do what?" she said.

"Run a successful funeral business."

"Oh," she said. "That."

"I liked your ceremony," I said. "For Maxine. I know I was being a little bitchy about it, but the truth is it was really nice. It was better than anything my dad has done. That's probably why he crawled into his shell."

I watched as a bag boy waited for an old woman to open the trunk of her enormous Monte Carlo. I kept talking.

"I think you did something really nice for that woman. And it seemed to actually help the family. I'm not sure my dad is there yet. How'd you learn to do it?"

My dad was coming out of the store now, carrying two heavy bags. He pretended they were too heavy and smiled like a goof.

"Why don't you come to my office?" Grace said. "My assistant can get us some coffee. We'll talk about it. When are you free?"

I laughed out loud.

"What's funny about that?"

"I've ruined my future," I said. "I got nothing but time."

"Come by this afternoon then," she said.

My dad was loading the bags in the trunk. What would he think if I was meeting with the enemy? Before I could respond, Grace spoke again.

"I'll see you at three," she said. "The address is on my card."

In the end, I lied to my dad.

What other choice did I have? I sat around half the afternoon trying to think about how I could get him to understand why I needed business advice from his rival. But when the time came, I just told him I needed a giant box of tampons. Then I drove my ugly car to a neighborhood full of art galleries where Grace had her office. When I got there, I stood in front of a big window that faced the avenue. There was a sign hanging just behind the glass that read:

WHAT IS A DEATHCARE MIDWIFE?

Beneath these words was a list of answers to a question that I hadn't asked:

AN ADVOCATE! We help you deal with anything you need in your time of loss, from legal paperwork to negotiation with area cemeteries and preserves!
A PLANNER! We arrange for in-home wakes and green burials outside of the traditional parlor system!
A STEWARD! We protect local ecological cycles and our planet as a whole with every decision we make!

A few too many exclamation points for my taste (!).

I had just finished reading it all when I heard the tap of fingernails on the glass. I looked past the sign to find a woman in square glasses staring back at me. I walked over to the door and stepped inside the modern office space.

"Miss Fowler?" the woman asked.

She squinted at me like I was out of focus.

"Yes," I said. "But . . ."

"You're early," she said.

"Right," I said. "That's why I was outside."

"I'll let Grace know you're here."

She walked away and I looked around the small space. Aside from a very tiny coffin display, with models made of wicker, bamboo, and other planet-friendly stuff, you'd never know anyone dealt with death in this place. It looked like the acupuncturist's office in Manhattan where my mom went.

Grace's office door swung open, and the woman with the square glasses ushered me inside. I found Grace standing behind her desk. Her hair was piled on top of her head, held together by a mass of bobby pins. She looked like the bohemian art teacher I'd had in elementary school, a woman who wore sandals in the dead of winter and talked to us about the transcendent sensuality in Picasso's early reclining nudes.

"Tess," she said. "Welcome to Greener Pastures."

"Thanks," I said. "It smells gardeny in here."

"We have a scent made for us," she said. "With cacao. That's probably what you're smelling."

"Maybe," I said.

Her office was just like the rest of the space. Sleek. Accents of wood. Green things budding from every surface.

"I'm afraid I only have a short time," Grace said. "I have to meet a family for a home ceremony this evening."

"You're having a funeral in their home?"

"It's one of our services."

I sat down in an uncomfortable chair across from her.

"Why would anyone want to do that?" I asked. "It sounds depressing as hell."

Grace wasn't fazed. She just sat down and adjusted a bobby pin.

"Tess," she said. "I think one of the reasons we're so scared of death in this country is because as soon as someone dies, the body is taken away and pumped full of chemicals. There's no direct contact with the dead anymore."

"Maybe that's a good thing."

"I'm not so sure. We used to be better at this. The body would stay with the family so they could wash and dress and care for it. They could have time alone with it to grieve and come to understand what happened."

I couldn't help thinking about Jonah, and the fact that I had never seen his body, let alone touched it. I had barely seen it when he was alive.

"But maybe it's okay not to see it," I said. "Maybe it would just be too hard, you know? Maybe you're forcing people to do things they don't want to do."

"I don't force people to do anything, Tess," she said. "I give them options."

The woman with the square glasses came in and poured two cups of coffee in glass mugs and then disappeared behind a nearly slammed door.

"Your assistant is a real people person," I said.

"Oh, Morgan's okay," said Grace. "She just knows who you are. That's all."

I took a long drink of coffee.

"And who am I exactly?"

"She's heard the story. She doesn't think I should be staying in contact with you. She thinks you're going to sue me or something."

"So she thinks I'm mentally disturbed?"

"Well, you did jump in a freezing lake with all your clothes on."

I tried not to laugh, but the image was suddenly too ridiculous. A lone chuckle escaped.

"Listen, Tess," she said, her face getting serious. "It's a little weird between us. I can deal with that, okay? But I just want to tell you something before you go."

"I'm listening," I mumbled.

"I know you're mourning someone," said Grace.

I opened my mouth to deny it.

"I know the signs," she said. "I've been doing this a while now."

"What are you talking about?" I said.

She gave me a look that said: Please cut the crap.

"I lost someone, too," she said.

"What?"

"A child," she said.

I tried to stay calm, but my palms were starting to sweat.

"About three years ago," she said.

"How?" I managed.

"She had a genetic disease. Neurological."

"How old was she?"

"Twenty-two months."

When she had said a child, she had meant a child.

"Grace," I said, "I'm sorry. I . . ."

Her eyes were dry, but her brow was folded tight. She was quiet for a minute. Then she began to speak.

"After it happened, I wanted every happy person in the

world to be as miserable as I was. I wanted everyone to experience a tragedy like mine. Otherwise I couldn't talk to them again. I couldn't relate to anything about them."

"Okay," I said.

"But a little later, maybe a year or so, I wanted something different. I wanted people to be able to say goodbye the way I had. It was the only good thing, really, that we got to do it on our terms. Someone helped us out, and we kept her at the house. I wanted to help other people in the same way. You came here for business advice, right?"

When she looked at me this time, I wasn't sure I could keep anything from her.

I nodded.

"Well, that's the best advice I can give you. Make sure you and your dad are not compromising. Do things the way you want them to be done. The way that feels important and right to you and your clients. That's all you have. And it *can* make a difference. It made one for me."

There was a silence after that. And again, I wasn't sure what to say. I looked at her hands on the desk.

"Is that why you're not married anymore?" I asked.

She opened her eyes and looked at her ringless finger.

"He wasn't exactly supportive of the business."

"Too morbid?"

"*Obsessed* is the word he used."

Grace seemed slightly calmer now, but her face was still flushed.

"But I think it's okay to be obsessed for a little while," she said. "You can't just run away from your grief. You have to deal with it head on. No matter how difficult and strange it is."

We both took a drink of coffee.

"There are no shortcuts," she said. "You have to do the hard stuff before it gets any easier."

19

Things I'm Seeing Without You:

Me: A completely dark bedroom in Minnesota. All I have to do is turn on the bedside lamp, stare at it intently for ten seconds, and then switch it off, and I can make everything go away. Poof! When the afterimage has wobbled off, there is nothing there but complete blackness.

Me: Even with my eyes open, I can see nothing. And it feels, for a moment, like I'm part of that nothing. I can't help asking you, Jonah: Is this what being dead feels like? Is it really as dark and empty as we think? Or is it silly for me even to pretend I can know?

When I was young, I used to pray every night.

My family's not religious, so it was kind of a dirty secret. And my prayer was not the regular kind. It was more of a neurotic laundry list. I decided at some point that if I didn't mention all of my family members and friends in my prayers, they would come to some harm in the night.

A falling piano would come crashing through their ceiling to squash them. Or God would pick them up and flick them into outer space with his enormous fingers just to punish me for my lack of devotion. I also had to bless the room I was in, object by object ("And bless you, clothes hamper") or I couldn't get to sleep.

At some point I stopped all of this—I can't remember when—but the habit of chatting with someone in the dark is a hard one to break. Which is why I was still talking to Jonah in my head, I guess. Even though I could create total blackness in my room, my thoughts always seemed to glow in the dark. And sometimes the only way to get them to dim was to tell them to someone else.

Which is probably what led me to dig out my phone and dial a number that had been sitting in my "recent calls" box for a few days. I listened to the ringing, so loud in the silence of the night, and when I heard an answer, I didn't say hello. Instead I said:

"Tell me what he was like."

And though it had been days since we had last spoken, and though it was three in the morning, Daniel did not seem angry. He just seemed a little confused.

"I thought we weren't going to talk again," he said.

"Did you hear me?" I said.

Daniel sighed.

"I heard you," he said. His voice sounded tired. "But I'm not sure I can tell you."

"Because you don't want to?"

He dropped one of his signature pauses.

"Because I still don't know which was the real Jonah. The first one or the last one."

I knew by this point that just because Daniel was done speaking for the moment, it didn't mean he was done speaking for good. And sure enough, this time was no exception.

"I'd like to think that when he was on his medication, that was the real him. That was the best version. But later, when he was off it, I can't really deny that was him, either. It's hard to separate them."

"Okay then," I said. "Start with the one I met."

"The one you met," said Daniel, "was the closest thing I've ever had to a best friend."

He paused for longer than usual this time, so long that I asked: "You still there?"

He was and he started to talk.

"On the first day in our room together, move-in day, Jonah sensed that I was nervous and . . . not very social.

Which was true, I guess. I'd never really been in a place like MIT before. My dad was in the air force. My mom got a trade degree.

"So, he took me out of our dorm room and we went around knocking on every door in the hall, like Jehovah's Witnesses. And when people opened up, he said, 'This is Daniel Torres. He seems really cool. You should probably be his friend.' I honestly don't think I would have talked to anyone if he hadn't done that. And it was so easy for him.

"He didn't even think of it as doing something nice for me. It was just what he thought he was supposed to do. That night, we played video games until two in the morning and made a frozen pizza. And he told me that he'd had some problems in high school, but he had decided to forget about all that and have an incredible year. And he asked was I willing to join him in that endeavor? That's what he said 'endeavor.'"

"Sounds nice," I said.

"I almost cried. I was worried about college, and who my roommate was going to be, and I had gotten this guy. It was kind of amazing."

"How long did it last?"

"A few months. I was never alone when I didn't want to

be. Wherever he was going, it was assumed I would come along. Study sessions. Dinner. Red Sox games. Or just long walks, which is what he liked to do best. When I asked him why, he quoted Thomas Jefferson: 'The sovereign invigorator of the body is exercise, and of all the exercises, walking is the best.' Really kind of dorky when you think about it. But he seemed so genuine."

"And that's when I met him right? During this time?"

"Yes."

"What did he say about me?"

I listened to Daniel take a few breaths and heard him rustle around in his bed.

"He said he had gone to Iowa and fallen in love with a girl who puked at a party. And that he was going to marry her."

"Did he tell you about our talks after that?"

"Sometimes."

"How did you feel about that?"

"I don't know. Happy, I guess."

"Were you jealous?"

Silence.

"It's more complicated than that."

"How? How is it more complicated?"

I wished I could keep my anger from flaring up just

once. But anytime I caught him justifying things, I felt like throwing the phone across the room.

"I was in love with him," he said.

I didn't hear his breath this time, on the other end. I got the feeling he might be holding it.

"What do you mean?"

He didn't answer.

"So, you're gay?"

"No. I mean, not really. I don't think so."

"But you were in love with another guy."

"I know. It wasn't really sexual, though. I just loved him and I wanted to be part of his life. And so I wanted to love you the way he loved you."

"That doesn't make any sense."

"I don't know how to explain it. I just cared about him so much that I felt like I cared for you, too, because you were part of him. You were part of that love. I know it's kind of messed up, but that's how I felt."

He stopped talking, but I found I had nothing to say. I didn't want to tell him that I understood. Maybe not the creepy part about loving me without meeting me. But just that you loved who you loved, even when it was weird. Maybe *because* it was weird. Like a person you'd met once at a party. A person you didn't really know at all.

"When he stopped taking his meds and everything started to fall apart, I didn't want this to fall apart, too. The thing with you. You understand? I wanted to save it."

"Okay. And after you'd saved it, what did you want then?"

"Then, I guess, I wanted to hold on to it."

"To me, you mean?"

"To you."

"By lying."

"Except I didn't think I was."

"I'm sorry. You weren't pretending to be someone else?"

"I was."

"So how were you not lying?"

"What if everything I said felt true?"

I held the phone tight against my face. Daniel's voice eventually broke through the semidarkness.

"I thought you were going to hang up on me," he said.

"Me too," I said.

"What else?" he said.

There was a little humor in his voice. Maybe because he knew there were never enough "what else's" to even the score, to forgive what he'd done. No matter how many details I knew about him, how many vulnerable moments he presented to me, there would never be a way to chip away at that first lopsided power dynamic. It couldn't be erased. Still, I felt the urge to try.

"Your phone takes pictures, right?" I said.

"It does . . ." he said. "Because I don't live in 1985."

"I want you to take your picture and send it to me."

"It's a little dark."

"Turn on a light, genius."

"Should I send it to you now?"

"I'm going to hang up," I said, "and then you're going to send it to me. But there's one last thing."

"What?"

"I want you to be naked in the picture."

More silence.

"It's only fair. I think you know that."

I didn't wait for a response. I just ended the call. And I fully expected that he would call right back and try to argue his way out of it. But he didn't do that. And as time passed at a rate of about an hour per second, I wondered maybe if it was better if he didn't do it.

It would give me a chance to break contact, to prove that he never really wanted to be on even ground with me. What does a true liar do, after all, when you ask him to stand naked?

My phone buzzed with a message. There was no text.

Just an eighteen-year-old boy, naked in the mirror, holding his phone in front of him. I realized as soon as I saw him that he didn't look the way I thought he might. Despite all Daniel had told me, I had imagined someone thin and rangy with strong facial features. Someone like Jonah. But of course he didn't look at all like this.

His skin was light brown, and his body was solid, a little stocky even. Like maybe he used to be overweight as a kid, but he'd worked hard to overcome it. There was dark hair across his chest, arms, legs, and groin. His chest was firm and so were his arms, and a small hard belly protruded just slightly above his penis (which hung, just nudging his right leg). He was looking directly at the mirror with squinty brown eyes and heavy dark brows.

I can't describe the shot as sexy. I know the rules of the naked selfie; I had looked at them online occasionally. Usually, the dudes were sitting on the edge of a bed with an erection, pushing their hips up a bit to make themselves look bigger. If not, then they were flexing in the mirror with their lips curled like smirking porn stars.

Daniel was just there, no affectation. No staging. Not that I'd really given him time for that kind of thing. But the effect was startling. It wasn't anything like the profile photos of Jonah I'd been looking at for the last year. It was just a naked guy in his room with an imperfect body. And it prompted me, finally, to turn off my phone. But not before another text came in and sat there in the palm of my hand.

WHAT ELSE?

20

The next day, I came downstairs for breakfast and found my dad more animated than I'd seen him in a decade. He was sitting at the table, doing twenty things at once. Looking at the paper, chewing his toast, bouncing his leg. I could barely focus on him. I would have been more concerned if I didn't recognize the energy. He was excited about a new idea.

"Morning, pardner!" he said when he saw me.

In the old days, he used to pitch schemes to my mom before she was even awake. Secretly, I think she found it a little exciting. Until all the ideas failed.

"How many cups of coffee have you had?" I asked.

"I lost count," he said. "Sit down. I want to tell you a story."

I sighed and rubbed the crusty sleep from my eyes. Then I poured some coffee and threw myself down into the chair across from him.

"I want to tell you about this guy I met when I first got started. Irving Breeze."

"That's not a real person," I said.

I grabbed a piece of toast from his plate and took a bite.

"Just listen. He owned his own funeral home in South Minneapolis for forty years. And it was incredibly successful, but not because there was anything exceptional about it. He buried people. He cremated people. He gave wakes and viewings. He was, quite literally, your grandmother's funeral director."

"Is this going somewhere?"

"The X-factor," said my dad, "was Irv himself. He was a former football player who liked to wink and shake hands, and he was the undisputed champion of the church potluck. He subscribed to the newsletters of every congregation in town and he scanned them every week for any event open to the public.

"It didn't matter what religion. He'd show up clutching a pan of hotdish or homemade Scotcheroos in his enormous hands. And on his way out, he'd always leave the man of the cloth with a wink, a donation, and a lovely notepad with the name of his parlor stenciled on the top. The next time one of the flock met their maker, guess which funeral home was recommended to the family?"

"Irv the Perv's?"

"Don't call him that."

His smile momentarily faltered.

"So, what do you think?" he asked.

"I'm down for crashing potlucks," I said, "but you don't know anything about church. They're going to smell the Godlessness on you."

"I don't want to go to churches," my dad said. "There's a larger message here, Tessie, if you would just listen for it. You can't just wait around. Sometimes, you have to drum up your own business. Even in the death industry."

His leg was bouncing like crazy now. I reached out and took the coffee mug from his hand. Then I waited and listened for the brilliant idea that was surely on its way.

"Nursing homes," he said.

I looked at him.

"Isn't that a little crass? Even for you?"

"No," he said.

I thought he was done speaking. Then he started up again.

"I remember when I was in the hospice with your grandma, one of the nurses was telling me that most of the residents didn't have a plan. They wanted one, but they weren't mobile enough to go to parlors. Their needs weren't being met. They might be our ideal customers,

Tess. Practical and quickly approaching their time of need!"

"I don't know . . ." I said. "It sounds kind of tacky."

"Just give it a chance," he said.

"Are you broke again or something?" I asked.

"I may have had some debts to pay with the Ocala money," he said.

I took a bite of toast and chewed it slowly.

"I'll think about it," I said.

"Great," he said. "I made an appointment at Sunrise Commons in an hour."

Sunrise Commons, as you might have guessed, was a new senior living place in the deep suburbs. And before we got there, we saw a billboard for it off the side of the highway: an enormous photo of a stylish older couple holding up sparkling wineglasses. Above them, a chandelier hung like an oversized halo. They looked like they were about to have athletic old-person sex any minute. And over their smiling faces in five-foot font, the board read: RETIRE . . . BUT NOT FROM LIFE!

"Damn," I said. "There goes your sales pitch."

When we actually got to the place, the grounds looked more like my old boarding school than a nursing home. It was all decorative cornices, porticoes, redbrick chimneys.

Maybe, I thought, it was a way to bring the old back to their youth. And sure enough, just after we got there, we were almost mowed down by a golf cart full of giggling octogenarians.

Inside, we walked past a fireplace bursting with spring flowers. The rest of the room was just as ornamented. Arched doorways. Wainscoting. At the front counter was a petite birdlike woman with dyed blond hair, and the largest, whitest teeth I've seen.

"Welcome to Sunrise Commons," she said. "How may I brighten your day?"

"We're here to give the death talk," I said.

The woman's face fell like it had been hit with a tranquilizer dart.

"I'm sorry," Dad said. "I'm Duncan Fowler. I'm giving the presentation about end-of-life care decisions. I believe it's in the Vanderplank Room."

The woman's shrewd stare was still stuck on my face as she tapped something into a touch screen on her desk.

"Fowler you said?"

Dad nodded. More tapping.

"Okay. Right. Yes. I see."

She examined both of us one more time and rose to her feet.

"Well, I guess you'd better come this way."

She set off walking, and my dad gave me a *what-the-hell* look. His manic energy had now been replaced by a Zen-like focus. We strolled through the main building of the commons, which was a maze of tiled hallways. Finally, we reached a wing in the back of the complex that actually looked and smelled like a real nursing home.

The decor was plain, and the scent of pureed food lingered in the air, melding with lemony disinfectant. When we stepped through the door of the common room, the assembled audience for Dad's talk looked like it was composed of the oldest living humans on earth.

So this was where they kept them.

Most were in wheelchairs. Some were sitting on couches with throw blankets folded neatly across their laps. The man closest to me wore a pair of glasses with one eye blacked out. Another woman had hair so wispy and delicate it looked like dandelion fluff that might blow away in a strong breeze. Dad turned to his new congregation, cleared his throat, and pulled out a handful of lined yellow note-cards.

"Good morning, everyone," he said. "Thank you for coming."

There were a few return blinks.

"My name is Duncan Fowler. Behind me is my daughter and business partner, Tess Fowler. We specialize in unconventional funerals. And today, I would like to talk to you about doing something truly spectacular with the end of your life."

A man in a stocking cap sniffled.

"It may seem a little odd to you, but I've come to realize that I care a lot about death rituals. Rituals for grief are some of the most important ones we have. And I'm trying to find ways to broaden the conversation about them."

He looked back at me. I nodded. He wasn't botching this, for once.

"What I really want to do is something meaningful, something that matches your personality. A ceremony that helps people feel like they have experienced something real about you."

The man with one visible eye had it open wide now.

"All of you have lived long lives, and I'm sure there are many people who love you. I know it would help them to have an opportunity to remember you when your time comes. So, if any of you would like help with your final arrangements, I'm willing to assist you in any way I can. That's why I'm here today."

I exhaled and looked around the room. Dad hadn't said

anything stupid. In fact, he had kind of nailed it. But the crowd might as well have been a still photograph. Finally, the one-eyed man adjusted his glasses and raised his hand.

"I have a question," he said.

Dad looked him in the eye and nodded. The man's face constricted in anger suddenly, as if some switch on his back had been flipped.

"Why can't you see that it's completely useless?" he yelled.

The room filled with institutional silence.

"I'm sorry," said my father. "What exactly?"

The man looked at him incredulously.

"The salad bar. It's useless. A waste of space. Why do we have to pay for that when nobody wants it here?"

A dark-haired attendant quickly came over and put her hand on the man's shoulder. She smiled.

"Okay, Mr. Cole," she said. "We all know your opinion on the salad bar by now."

"Dad . . ." I said.

"The real problem is," the woman with the fluffy hair chimed in, "is that my daughter is supposed to pick me up in an hour. But she's not going to know which room I'm in. Who can help me with *that*?"

I walked over to the attendant, a Latina woman with her hair tied back in a tight ponytail.

"What are they so upset about?" I said.

My dad stood next to me.

"Don't worry," she said. "It's not you. Most of these people are from the Memory Care unit. They have their good days and bad days."

"Memory care," I said. "As in . . ."

"Alzheimer's. Other forms of dementia. Many of these patients have a high level of impairment."

A few more people in the back had their hands up now. My dad looked at them.

"Why are they at my talk?" he asked.

"It's good to get them out of their rooms. They don't have a lot of outside interaction."

I stepped off to the side, wondering how quickly we could leave.

Then I saw the woman.

I'm not sure if she had been in the room before, or if she had just arrived during the Q&A. She had a bright white Betty Page haircut and a lip-sticky smile. It looked like she had gone directly from age nineteen into old age without anything in between. She was motioning me to the back row. When I reached her, she touched my wrist.

"I enjoyed the speech," she said. "My name is Mamie Lee."

I looked down at her. Her soft brown eyes darted back and forth.

"Thank you," I said. "I just need to get my dad, so . . ."

I started to move forward but she tugged on my shirt-sleeve.

"I would like to plan a funeral," she said.

"Okay," I said. "My dad has some forms I can leave with you. Maybe you can go over them with a family member."

"That's not what I want," she said calmly.

Dad was looking at us now.

"I would like to have my funeral in two weeks," she said.

I closed my eyes. I was starting to suspect the woman at the front desk of sabotage. When I opened my eyes again, Mamie Lee was looking right at me.

"I was just admitted here," she said. "I'm in the early stages, but I've seen it move fast, and that's how it usually works in my family. I would like to have one of your celebration funerals before I'm too far gone. Is that something you can do? Have it while you're still alive?"

I looked over at my dad. His mouth was open. He didn't seem capable of providing an answer, which wasn't surprising.

"Of course!" I said. "We . . . do that all the time."

I was not looking at my father now. Only Mamie Lee.

"Do you know what kind of celebration you want?" I asked.

The woman smiled to herself.

"Oh yes, darling," she said. "I would like a burlesque funeral."

And then I watched my father's face turn a shade I had never seen before.

21

"What the hell were you thinking? Saying yes without asking me?"

We were back in the parking lot of Sunrise Commons, watching the fake old people go about their days. Oh, and Dad was kind of pissed.

"Have you had a total meltdown, Tess? Is that what's happening?"

"I was drumming up business," I said. "I thought you'd be happy."

"I'm not happy," he said. "That room was full of people who barely know their own names. Now a woman wants to have a burlesque funeral. There are some ethical issues to consider here."

"Oh. You're ethical now? You were the one who wanted to prey on nursing homes in the first place. *I know, Tess. Let's go to the place where everyone's slowly dying and sell them some funerals!*"

"I'm pretty sure I didn't say that."

"Also, Mamie's different. You heard her describe the situation herself. She's fine right now."

"She wants people to take off their clothes at her funeral."

"We don't really know the details yet."

I watched as a robust old man left Sunrise with his golf clubs. He looked like a walking Viagra ad.

"She might have been having a rare lucid day, Tess," Dad said. "Tomorrow she could wake up with no idea what she said."

He opened the door to his Volkswagen, but he didn't get in. He just stood there between the door and the car.

"What's the point of a living funeral anyway?" he said. "It doesn't make any sense."

I stepped closer to him.

"Maybe what doesn't make sense is having a funeral when you're dead," I said.

"Give me a break, Tess."

"Seriously. Think about it for a second. Why have a party when you aren't going to be there to enjoy it? What sense does that make? You wouldn't have a birthday party and *not* go?

My dad got in the car then and sat behind the wheel.

"C'mon," he said. "We're leaving. This was a disaster."

I opened the door. He went to turn on the ignition, but I grabbed his hand.

"I mean it, Dad," I said. "Maybe she wants to have a celebration when she can actually see everyone she loves one last time? Mamie's not dead yet, but she's dying. She's losing the personality that she once had. That's a form of dying, anyway. And she knows it's happening. Why can't she celebrate the person she was before she's gone completely?"

My dad just sat there a minute, gripping the wheel. He tightened his lips.

"What if her family shows up and says I'm taking advantage of an impaired woman? Meanwhile, there are naked people dancing everywhere. That could be bad, Tess. I can't risk another lawsuit after Nantucket."

I looked at his face. It seemed like he was actually scared.

"You were all gung-ho this morning," I said. "What happened? When did you become such a pansy?"

"I'm done talking about this."

"Just let me meet with her again," I said.

He shook his head slowly, but he didn't look at me.

"She wants something outside the norm," I said. "Isn't that what we're in business to do?"

I waited for his answer, but it didn't come. He just started the car and drove us away without looking back.

■ ■ ■

My phone rang later that night.

I was up watching old-timey burlesque dancers on the Internet, which definitely beat my dad's *Playboy*s when it came to vintage porn. These women were bosses. There were no airbrushed nipples and cutesy little girl poses. The burlesque ladies shook and shimmied in spectacular clubs full of men in sharp suits. It seemed impossible that Mamie used to do this.

I picked up the phone.

"Was it that bad?"

Daniel's voice was sharper than usual.

"What?" I said.

He sighed.

"Tess, it's a little weird to send someone a naked picture and then not hear from them for an entire day."

"You must be crushed," I said. "Do you feel betrayed? Like you put yourself out there and got nothing back?"

"I see what you're doing," he said.

I looked away from the computer and listened for Daniel's breath.

"It wasn't bad," I said.

"What?"

"Your picture."

"Oh."

"Yeah."

"Huh."

"So . . . Yeah."

There was another pause.

"I guess we've seen each other naked now," I said.

He was quiet. But the air felt charged with something suddenly. I didn't want it to be, but I couldn't make it stop. We didn't say anything for ten seconds or so. Then I asked the first thing that came to mind.

"How did he do it?"

Another silence. I heard Daniel breathing on the phone.

"Pills," he said finally. "The ones he hadn't been taking. You didn't know?"

"No. Not the details. I never really tried to find out."

I closed my eyes.

"They tried to pump his stomach," he said, "but it was too late. He was unconscious in the bathroom in our hall and the RA couldn't bring him back."

I lay my head down on my father's desk.

"Did you have any idea?" I asked. "That he was capable of that?"

"I don't know. If I didn't live with him, I never would have suspected anything. I knew he wasn't going to class, and eventually I found out he wasn't taking his meds. But right when I was really starting to get worried, he seemed to get better. I thought he was getting back to normal. The only sign was the park thing."

"Park thing?"

Daniel took a deep breath.

"It's kind of a whole long story."

"Tell me," I said.

Another breath.

"We were on one of our walks," he said. "Even when he wasn't feeling great, he still wanted to walk. And on this day, he said he wanted to go to the Public Gardens. He used to go there with his family on vacation when he was a kid. *Make Way for Ducklings* and all that. So we walked across the bridge from campus. There had been a lot of rain lately, and I remember the Charles River was really high. We stopped to watch it from the bridge, and the current seemed so much faster than usual.

"There were no boats out even though it was sunny. Jonah was in a decent mood, and he was telling me about the history of the Charles, how it used to be so full of sewage that people who fell in had to get tetanus shots. I wasn't really listening to him, though. I was watching his face to see if it looked more like the Jonah I knew. And there was something there. His eyes seemed to have more life to them.

"We walked into the gardens, and I followed Jonah to the Lagoon Bridge. The Swan Boats weren't going yet, but they were parked against the banks. We sat down on a bench near one of the weeping willows. Jonah had been talking a lot, but suddenly he got really quiet. And I noticed he was distracted, looking at something on the other side of the lagoon.

"Somehow I had missed it, but almost directly across from us there was this homeless guy sitting there, dressed in multiple layers of sweaters and suit coats. I couldn't see his face because he had a hood pulled tight over his head. But I could see a gray beard spilling over his chest. And he was surrounded on all sides by these giant blue translucent garbage bags full of white stuff. He must have had six or seven of these bags, each one full to bursting.

"After he got settled, he opened one up and reached his hand inside. Then he brought it out and threw a fistful of the white stuff in the air. It rained down in clumps onto the water and the grass surrounding him. And suddenly, it was like a signal had been sent to every bird in the park at once. They all descended on the same spot like vultures.

"It was bread, of course, the white stuff. Wonder Bread. And once he started flinging it, he didn't stop. Sometimes he shredded the slices with his hands. Sometimes he chucked them whole. Soon, we couldn't even see him anymore for all the dive-bombing birds. Ducks. Pigeons. Seagulls. Crows. It was a battle royal, which was ridiculous because it was clear he was never going to run out of bread. He had enough to feed every bird in the park until they were stuffed. He was the god of bread.

"When I looked over at Jonah, I noticed that he was crying. And not just a little. There were tears pouring down his face. He stood up and told me he couldn't be there anymore. And I put my arm around him and walked with him until we had left everything behind. The park. And the lagoon. And the old man with the bread. I tried talking about it at first. 'Where did he even get all the bread?' I asked. But he was silent. So I asked him what was wrong, and he couldn't explain it to me. It was only after we'd been walking a while that he looked me in the eye. And he said, 'I just know how that guy feels.'

"But he wouldn't say anything else about it. When we got back to campus he seemed okay again. He calmed down and he apologized for his breakdown in the park. He even laughed about it a little. I told him I thought maybe he should see somebody at Health Services, a counselor, and he assured me he would. He told me I was a good friend and that he was lucky he knew me. And then we played video games for a couple of hours and went to bed like it was any other day.

"I felt better the next day, like maybe I had gotten through to him. But, after that, he wasn't around the room very much. Then he disappeared for a couple of days, and I never saw him again."

I wiped my runny nose on my sleeve. I had started crying at some point, but I wasn't sure when.

"What happened after that?" I asked.

"My parents flew out and came to campus the next day. They moved me to a hotel by the airport. I made them stay around for a week, but nothing really happened. A vigil outside. A moment of silence in the cafeteria. A discussion about suicide prevention education. Then we went home."

"What about the funeral?"

"There was no funeral."

His voice was softer now.

"It was just a private thing for the family. I called his mom the day after it happened, and asked if I could come. She said no."

"Did she say why?"

"She said it would be too much. Too painful to see her son's friends, other people his age. She apologized, but she couldn't do it. There was a charity set up somewhere. I could donate to that if I wanted."

"So you never saw his body?"

"No."

"What about when it actually happened?"

"By the time I heard, they had already taken him away."

I nodded, even though I knew he couldn't hear that through the phone.

"Before my parents got there I was in our dorm room by myself. And I found this folder he had kept. Inside it was a list of things he was going to do when he got better. It was from a self-help book or something. Some of them were simple like 'get a part-time job.' Others were a little more Jonah: 'learn to be a projectionist at a revival movie house.' But the one that stuck out to me was 'study away in Sicily.' It's not that big a deal, I guess. A lot of college kids study abroad. But there was something about picturing him in another country that just brought it all home. If things had gone a different way, I could imagine him there so easily."

"Why didn't anyone else know about his depression? Why wasn't someone else there to stop him?"

Daniel sighed.

"He didn't have any other good friends, Tess," he said.

"Everybody liked him, but not many people knew him. I think we were it. You and me. We were all he had."

"That can't be true," I said.

"Can you see why I didn't want it to end?" said Daniel.

I sat up suddenly. The phone was wet and hot against my ear.

"I can't do this," I said.

Daniel's voice sounded desperate when he spoke.

"Tess," he said.

"No," I said. "I mean. *This*. The distance. The phone. I can't do this kind of thing anymore. I don't think it's good for me."

He was silent for a moment.

"So, what are you saying exactly?" he said.

I debated for a second about whether to speak the sentence in my mind. It was just hovering there, waiting to change everything. But I couldn't hold it back. It seemed like the only thing left to do.

"What I'm saying is," I said, "no more phones."

22

I went back to Sunrise the next day.

I worried about what to tell my dad, but when I woke up he wasn't there. I'd heard him talking on the phone the night before, giggling like an idiot, but that was the only thing out of the ordinary. So I drove back to the commons and showed up during visiting hours. When I got back to the Memory Care Unit, I immediately saw two men get into a screaming match over a game of Connect Four. They had to be sent to their rooms like children. I started to wonder if I had it in me to hang around this place.

This all changed when I found Mamie.

"Tilly!" she called to me, when I showed up.

"Hi, Mamie," I said.

I didn't correct her about my name. Though, what my dad said about her lucidity flashed through my brain.

"Come with me," she said. "It's my day in the salon. I've got to get my hair set!"

She took me down to the on-site hair salon, and soon her head was full of pink curlers. I wasn't sure how to start talking to her about her funeral. But she jumped right in. Before we could move forward with the planning, she said, I needed to know something about burlesque. So Mamie Lee started to tell her story.

"I left Minnesota for Hollywood first," she said. "But after doing some work in the chorus lines, a promoter saw me and thought I'd be good for his club in New York. He told me I could have top billing if I didn't mind showing a little more."

She blushed, but just for a second.

"You have to understand, though, Tilly. It's not like it is now with girls showing everything down there and working on greasy poles. It was glamorous! A show. And it was about the tease. At Minsky's, I once took two whole minutes to remove a glove! The guys went crazy for it. They jumped out of their seats! What do you think happened when they saw my bazooms?!"

I started recording Mamie on my cell phone camera, so I could remember some of this. I focused on the little flip of her white hair with her manicured hand. If she noticed my recording, she didn't seem to care.

"There were a lot of men," she went on. "But I never

went in for the comedians. I was into the sax players myself. They wailed on the stuff that got us going crazy. And there was this one player who was so nervous around me. I used to look him in the eye while he was playing and wait for him to miss a note. Once I left my pasties on his dressing room door. He was just a boy, really. I missed him when I quit performing, but I never did talk to him again."

"Why'd you give it up?" I asked.

For a moment, Mamie looked like a statue of herself, sitting there, completely still. Then she spoke out of the corner of her mouth.

"It wasn't really my choice, sweetie," she said. "I couldn't make the jump to the movies. Couldn't act for a damn."

"But you could have still danced, right?"

The skinny blond doing her hair spritzed Mamie's curls with a spray bottle. The sunlight caught the mist and made it glow around her head.

Mamie didn't answer my question.

"Do you still have your old costumes and everything?" I asked.

Mamie waved her hand like she was shooing away a fly.

"I sent what was left to Exotic Land, years ago."

I watched her eyes droop closed in the long salon mirror.

"Exotic Land?"

"Burlesque Hall of Fame out there in Vegas. They got Sheri Champagne's ashes, I hear. And Jane Mansfield's sofa, shaped like a heart."

"Have you kept in touch with any of the girls?"

She shook her head. I saw Mamie's eyes go moist. The hairdresser glared at me.

"We try to keep them from getting upset," she said, as if Mamie wasn't able to hear her.

"Sorry," I said. "I didn't mean to upset anybody."

I shut off my phone. But Mamie spoke up.

"Leave it on," she said.

"I'm sorry?" I said.

"Your little camera gadget. Go ahead and leave it on if you want. It's okay."

She turned toward the hairdresser.

"You can set me in a minute, Jordan."

The hairdresser puffed out a breath and walked away. I turned my phone back on and leveled it on Mamie Lee's face.

"I didn't want to give it up," she said. "There's the truth."

She wiped a tear from the top of her cheekbone.

"I married a man from back here, a friend of the family, and he told me I was through with it. He was real conservative. Nice enough, but manipulative. I learned too late that's the worst quality in a man. He wanted to reform me, I guess. That was his kick."

"Why didn't you say no?"

"I didn't know what options I had. It was hard to get a straight job afterward, so I came back to become a housewife. I guess I was comfortable enough, but I always regretted giving everything up so quick and not keeping up with the girls. My husband died a few years ago and left me some money. I'd like to put some of it toward something a little wicked. You understand me, Tilly?"

"Yes," I said. "I do."

"I spent too much of my life being good. It's killing me."

I turned off my camera. I squeezed her hand and told her I would be back soon with a plan. Then I walked out of the commons, my thoughts already churning. Who would even attend Mamie's ceremony if we could pull it off? She told me she wasn't close with her children and she had very little other family.

I was driving back, playing my recording in the car, when the answer came to me. And when it did, I found myself pulling over to look up a number and make a call to a place I hoped actually existed.

23

Daniel didn't call that night. Or the night after.

Of course, I had told him not to, but I was still surprised when he didn't. I knew the last thing I told him had been an ultimatum of sorts. And I knew it had been abrupt. But I didn't care. I was growing closer to yet another person I didn't really know. And I was trying to put an end to that stage of my life.

I'd already gone that route once and now that person, who had never really let me in, was gone for good. That's why my computer was at the bottom of a lake, confusing the hell out of local bottom-dwellers. That's why I was home planning funerals instead of getting a high school diploma.

And I needed to get better, not worse. So, I decided I wouldn't call again, even if I was tempted. I would let him go if that's what it took. And in the meantime, I would try everything I could not to think about him.

Instead, I would concentrate on Mamie's funeral. Now

that I'd heard her story, I knew I had to help her whether my father was on board or not. But in order to do it, I had two big problems to solve. The first was finding a venue. And the second was getting in touch with Mamie's old friends.

I started with the first.

Unfortunately, my early attempts were a bust. Sunrise Commons refused to do anything related to funerals or stripping, let alone a combo of the two. Funeral homes preferred dead bodies to half-naked living ones. And community centers seemed to have a limited definition of a "community event." So late that morning, I went to the only other place I could think of: a strip club.

By noon I was standing outside of a place called Harry Palmer's. It was a dive, which is why I chose it. I had to have a better chance at a place so run down. Also, according to horny high school boys I'd once known, HP's was notorious about not carding. So, it came as a bit of a surprise when a man in a plaid Western shirt and a leather vest stopped me at the door.

"Not so fast, honey," he said. "Where do you think you're going?"

"To see some sad naked women?" I said.

He blinked. It appeared that he had never heard this

answer before. He scrunched his thick gray eyebrows.

"You have to be twenty-one," he muttered. "And all ladies need a male escort."

"I was just kidding," I said. "I don't want to see any boobs. I'm Harry's niece. I need to talk to him."

The man looked deeply perplexed now. He turned around, presumably to look for Harry. The leather tassels on his vest swished.

"Wait here," he said.

He lumbered across the room, and entered a door to the side of the stage. Immediately, I walked into the place and took a seat at a bar, which was strung with blinking red Christmas lights. I glanced toward the stage.

Thankfully, there weren't any girls my age working the day shift. The women dancing seemed chosen to appeal to an older clientele. Both dancers—one a dyed redhead with gravity-defying fake boobs and a thin Korean woman dressed like a stereotypical schoolgirl—looked old enough to be my mom. Or my mom's mom.

"You are not related to me!" came a voice from across the club. "And I don't need any new girls. Especially not under-age girls. That is not something I'm interested in."

A man I could only assume was Harry Palmer came up behind the bar, holding a Bloody Mary with half a garden stuffed inside. He had thick black hair sticking out of a faded military cap. When he smiled, he revealed a perfectly straight row of wine-stained teeth beneath his mustache.

"I suppose you could be a hostess," he said. "But that's the best I can do. The tips are still pretty good. But you have to deal with the regulars."

He took a long pull on his Bloody Mary.

"I'm not here for a job," I said.

He swallowed.

"Oh," he said. "Then it seems my drinking has been interrupted for no reason. Have a nice day. Francis will show you out."

He got up to walk away. The man in the Western shirt—Francis?—took a step forward. I wasn't sure what to say, so I tried to think about what a real businesswoman would do. Someone like Grace.

"Hey!" I said. "I don't intend to waste your time, Harry."

He turned around.

"No? Then why are you still sitting here?"

"Because I have a proposal that I think you might be interested in."

Harry crossed his arms and put on his professional look of interest. It was very similar to his regular look.

"Lay it on me," he said. "You have thirty seconds."

I waved my arm, gesturing toward the clients of the club.

"How many people do you typically get in here on a Monday morning?" I asked.

Harry pursed his lips and blew a long, wet raspberry.

"I figured," I said. "What if I told you I could fill this place with respectable people from the golden age of burlesque. The only thing you would have to do is give me the space. You keep everything from the bar. I cater, decorate, and organize."

He looked at me again, maybe for the first time.

"How old are you?" he said.

"Twenty," I said.

It was hard for me not to crack a smile, but I kept it together.

"What's the catch?" Harry asked.

"The catch is that it's a living funeral," I said.

I couldn't tell if the phrase meant anything to him. Or if he'd even heard me. Harry looked around his club, his gaze lingering on his clients. There was a man in cutoff jean shorts and cowboy boots, nursing a double-shot of whiskey. Another guy by the stage had a dollar in his teeth and a trucker hat that read "I Love Fat Chicks."

"Hell," said Harry. "Every day here is a living funeral."

24

**Here lies the last text
you'll ever get from me.**

This was the final dispatch from the land of Daniel Torres. It appeared on my phone at exactly 9:33 the next morning while I was eating breakfast by myself. My dad was off again, who knows where, so I had no one to tell me not to check my phone at the table. I was deciding whether to respond when UPS showed up on the porch with a heavily insured package. I brought it inside and looked at the label: Exotic Land, USA.

I'd spent the latter half of yesterday on the phone with the curator, telling her about Mamie. I even sent her the cell phone video of Mamie telling her story. She said she'd overnight me something, and I wasn't sure I believed her. But when I opened the box, I found a perfectly preserved black satin strapless gown, encrusted with thousands of glittering rhinestones.

The stones were incandescent in the light of the morning. They were like a constellation plunging down the dark satin bodice to a ruched waistline. The dress came with matching mid-length silver gloves, a fringed pair of black panties, and tasseled rhinestone pasties. Also included in the package were the names and contact information of ten living dancers from the golden age of burlesque.

I got on the phone right away, and called them up one-by-one. I spoke with a former Broadway actress first, a woman with a breathy voice who got into the trade when she couldn't get acting work. She was now a retired theater teacher in Arizona. I talked to a pinup girl who lived in a double-wide with all her memorabilia, the sole curator and visitor of her own mobile museum. "I remember Mamie," she croaked. "Great rack on that little lady!"

I talked to a woman once arrested for indecency who volunteered for her church these days. She'd danced with live cockatiels on both arms until one of the birds attacked someone at a show and she had to give them up. I talked to two dancers who never threw in the towel. They still performed on the revival circuit, jumping out of clam shells at the age of eighty-nine.

In the end, I got five out of the ten to confirm. Three others were maybes. Two were too sick to make it. Still, it was a start. I decided to take a ride out to Sunrise Commons to share the good news with Mamie.

It was a perfect spring day, and on the way, I rolled down all the windows and took deep breaths of fresh air until my mind felt temporarily defogged. It wasn't until I got to the parking lot of the home that I remembered Daniel's message. Now that it was in front of me, I wanted to write back. It would be so easy to dash off a text. Instead, I pressed a button and my screen went dark. Then I grabbed the dress and went inside.

When I got to the reception desk, I was told Mamie was not available because she was "recovering."

"What are you talking about?" I asked the woman with the giant teeth. "Recovering from what?"

"Mamie left the grounds yesterday," she said. "She wandered to a diner five miles from here. On the way back, she had a fall."

"What kind of fall?"

"I'm sorry," the woman said. "Are you family?"

"She hates her family," I said.

"I'm going to have to ask you to leave," she said.

I just stood there for a few minutes in the lobby after that, watching the receptionist tap away at her touch screen, as if everything were completely normal. Eventually, though, I told her I needed to use the restroom. Then, I headed down the hallway toward the restroom where I took a jagged left turn toward the passageway to Memory Care.

Mamie's door was closed, but it wasn't locked, and when I stepped inside, I was surprised to find no one on duty. Instead, I found the shades pulled and the lights off. I had to wait for my eyes to adjust to the dark before I could find the bedside light, and when I flipped it on, I got my first look at Mamie in the shadows.

She was on an IV and there was a large bandage across her forehead. Her hair and makeup weren't done, and I could finally see the age in her face: the thick lines from her mouth to the bottom of her chin, the loose cheeks and heavy-lidded eyes. I set the dress down on a chair and moved closer. Mamie's pupils opened to the room.

"It's you," she said in a hoarse voice.

I sat down on the bed and put my hand over Mamie's, which was cool and soft.

"Oh, Tilly," said Mamie, "I'm afraid I've made a mess of things."

I squeezed her hand.

"You don't need to apologize for anything," I said.

I picked up Mamie's hand and saw that her fingernails were speckled with patches of old nail polish. Either she had gone without a manicure, or she'd scratched them in the fall.

"I'm not supposed to have visitors," she said. "They even turned my husband away."

Her husband, I remembered, was no longer alive.

"It's okay," I said. "They told me I could stay."

I got up and prowled around Mamie's dresser, looking over her beauty supplies. She had never completely left the glitz of her dancing days behind, even in assisted living. And sure enough, at the base of the mirror, there was a row of candy-colored nail polish.

I picked the one that looked the brightest and made my way back over to the bed. I lifted her hand and held it gently. Then I uncapped the nail polish and began to apply a rich red coat to her right thumb.

"Here is what's going to happen," I said. "You are going to be strong for three more days. That's the soonest I think I can get things together. But I'm going to do it. It's going to happen."

I moved from Mamie's thumb to her pointer finger, painting as delicately as I could, but my hand wouldn't stop shaking. Mamie looked up at me. I kept talking.

"There's going to be a big party, full of all your friends, and it's going to be scandalous and amazing and nothing bad is going to happen because sometimes everything is perfect."

I painted the rest of the row and blew on Mamie's fingers. Mamie rested her unpainted hand on my back. And when I looked at her, it was hard to tell how present she was. There was something glassy about her gaze.

"Will you put it on?" she asked.

I looked around.

"My dress," she added. "The one you brought. I want you to try it on."

I glanced over at the dress, draped on the arm of a chair. I'd never even seen Mamie look at it.

"I brought it for you," I said.

"I know," said Mamie. "I want to remember what I looked like."

It took me a moment to understand what she meant, but it came to me soon enough. I walked over to the chair where I'd set the gown. Then I went into Mamie's small bathroom and took off the jeans and tank top I'd been wearing. In the cramped room, I raised my arms and pulled the filmy dress down over my body.

It was a little big in the chest, but otherwise it fit well. It made me look like I had an hourglass figure for the first time in my life. I glanced at myself in the mirror, made sure the zipper was tight, and came back into the room. Mamie looked at me when I appeared. She smiled.

"I remember attaching each of those stones," she said. "I did each one by hand."

I felt my eyes widen.

"You made this?"

"My mom taught all of us to sew. I thought I'd save a buck. I made all my own gowns. This one was my favorite, though. I wore it the last time I performed."

I moved closer to her and watched Mamie reach a hand out and touch the material. She closed her eyes as she rubbed it between the thumb and forefinger of the hand without the polish, maybe envisioning her last dance, maybe just relishing the sensation of the glossy fabric.

"Thank you, dear," she said.

"For what?" I asked.

"For the funeral party."

Her voice was so soft now I could barely hear her.

"We haven't had it yet," I said. "It's in three days. Remember?"

Mamie's eyes closed again, and she smiled.

"No," she said. "I was there. It was wonderful."

I stood there and watched her slowly drift to sleep.

Moments later, a nurse barged in and shooed me out. She said they were moving Mamie back to the hospital. Something new had shown up on the CT scan. I asked to come along, but I wasn't allowed. So, I could only watch from a distance as they loaded up Mamie on a gurney and wheeled her away.

I remembered I was still wearing the dress on my way back to the parking lot, which explained the odd looks I got from the staff. My other clothes were left behind in Mamie's room, but it was too late to go back and get them now. So I drove home in a decades-old burlesque costume, this time getting goose bumps from the breeze through the car, as the blue sky and fields blurred around me.

In the house, I found my father sitting at the kitchen table eating a sandwich. He gave me a double take in the dress, but made no immediate comment. There was a guilty look on his face, and his clothes looked a little disheveled. I poured myself some burnt coffee from the pot that had likely been on all morning. I could feel him watching me.

"What's going on?" he said.

I wasn't able to speak for a moment. There weren't clear words for what I was feeling. The closest I could come was: "There's no such thing."

My dad's mouth was still half open. There was a small piece of lettuce between his lower front teeth. He put his hand on my shoulder and then took it off again.

"I don't understand," he said.

"Closure," I said.

I wiped my eyes with the back of my hand, but it didn't help. The tears were coming now, like it or not, and I was quickly becoming a slobbering fool.

"We can't do a living funeral for Mamie," I said. "And I just wanted it so badly. She deserved it. But it's not going to happen."

My face was smashed against my father's sweater now, against the rough fibers that scratched against my forehead. His arms were around me. They were long and clumsy, but I was happy to have them there.

He didn't ask me any more questions. He just sat absolutely still and let me cry for the next few minutes. It was something he had always been good at, knowing when *not* to say something. When I removed my face from his shoulder there was a damp spot there. I looked up at him and calmed my voice.

"There's not really any closure," I said. "Is there?"

"I don't know, Tess," he said.

"So, then what's the point of what we do?" I asked. "If we can't provide that."

"Well . . ." he said. He handed me a napkin for my tears. "Maybe part of it's just to reaffirm to people."

"Reaffirm what?"

He looked away and scratched his chin, covered in black and gray stubble. Then he met my eyes again, and for once he didn't look like a sad clown. He looked serious.

"That we don't need as much closure as we think we do."

25

Mamie Lee died a day and a half later. When she fell, she had fractured her skull above the ear and torn an artery. Her brain was beginning to swell even when she spoke to me that last afternoon. By the time they brought her in for surgery the swelling was irreversible. She died in a coma, and later that day my dad was notified that she had left money behind for her funeral and she wanted his business to plan it.

"Tess," he said when he showed up to my room, "I don't know what to say."

"Say you're sorry."

"For what exactly?"

"For not taking Mamie seriously," I said. "And please just tell me you want to do this right."

He leaned against the doorframe.

"Okay. How is it going to work?"

I told him about Harry Palmer's.

"Jesus," he said. "You went to that place by yourself?"

"Harry is a shrewd businessman," I said.

"I wish you would have told me," he said.

"I bet you do."

Eventually Dad apologized and acquiesced to my demands. We would fly Mamie's old friends in and fix up Palmer's to look like a New York burlesque club. If it took all the money she set aside, then so be it.

So, in the days before the funeral we painted the walls red and put up silk curtains in the strip club. Then my dad hired a handyman, and they built a makeshift runway with a few theater seats around it. The only illumination came from footlights to accentuate the legs of the performers. "They're the last to go!" proclaimed Candy, an aging dancer with hair dyed the color of a blood orange. She showed up from the airport at five in the morning.

Because of the short notice, the crowd was smaller than I hoped. Besides the old burlesquers there was only me, my dad, Harry Palmer, and a few of the younger strippers from his club. And, of course, the body of Mamie herself, displayed in the corner, bathed in a magenta spotlight.

She was in the rhinestone dress, and we hired one of the best makeup artists in town to make her look like she was about to go onstage. She had dark-lined cat eyes, long spidery lashes, and glittering bright red lipstick. Her white Betty Page haircut was side-swept along her face in waves.

Onstage was Lillian Orlando. She was telling a story about the time she and Mamie caused a car crash, crossing the street to get Chinese food in their stage costumes. Then her song came on, and she did a memorial fan dance to a big band tune. For ten minutes she eclipsed two black feathered fans across her body, strutting above the floodlights, ending the number entirely hidden behind the plumes of her veil.

It was all really beautiful, I guess.

I mean there's something undeniably soul-lifting about elderly exotic dancers shaking it for their fallen comrade. But I couldn't quite slough off my sadness. The fact remained: Mamie never got to see this. She died without a reunion, without a chance to be who she most wanted to be again.

After a while, I decided to escape to the bathroom for a minute to catch my breath. When I approached the restroom door, however, it swung open and out walked a woman in stylish mourning gear. Even without getting a good look, I knew instantly who it was.

"Grace," I said. "What are you doing here?"

Grace fiddled with her hair and looked around the room.

"Attending the burlesque funeral of Mamie Ann Lee," she said. "I heard you did most of the planning on this one. Congratulations. It looks great."

"Thanks," I said.

Oddly enough, I was glad she was there. If I was being honest with myself, some of her advice from that day at her office had guided me. I was about to say something when she looked around again with an anxious gaze.

"Did you know Mamie?" I asked.

"Oh, no," she said.

Her eyes were still scanning the room. I waited until her eyes came back to me.

"Then how did you find out about this?"

"Your father," she said.

She spoke quickly, and I almost didn't hear her.

"What about him?"

The skin around her freckles was turning pink.

"He invited me. We've been . . . corresponding a little."

My father came across the room just then.

"Grace," he said. "You made it!"

Then he turned to me.

"Tessie," he said. "I hope you don't mind. I thought Grace should get a look at the competition, now that we're ramping up our efforts."

He smiled his charming, goofy smile, and rested his hand on her forearm, ever so briefly.

"I'm sorry," I said. "I just need a moment."

The humid club was closing in on me. It seemed very clear, suddenly, that Grace had only taken an interest in me to get close to my supposedly dreamy, single father. So I walked away from the restrooms and stepped outside into the cool of the evening in order to be less aware of this fact for a moment.

Still it stung. Was I going to go the rest of my life thinking anyone who showed any interest in me was my best friend? Was I going to be the last person to understand what was actually happening to me every time? An entire life like that seemed like the most exhausting thing imaginable.

Harry Palmer's was by the railroad tracks, and there was a large freighter inching by about twenty feet away. Each car's graffiti was more vibrant than the last's. It was an unending colorful sentence full of odd words I didn't understand. J-FISH. BOWLER. NADA-NADA. FUGUE. I wondered for a moment if it was a message just for me. My phone buzzed.

Don't go back inside.

I stared down at the sentence from Daniel. My heart started beating in my ears.

Inside where?

The train clacked by, but it sounded like it was running inside my head.

I think you know.

I looked up from my phone, and in the space between the cars, I saw the outline of a figure. I waited until the last car had rumbled past, and then the person was walking toward me. It was a person that, up until now, I had only seen naked. Today, he was in a T-shirt and jeans, a backpack hanging off his right shoulder on a single strap, and a worn baseball cap on his head.

He took his time moving across the tracks. Then he stopped a few feet in front of me. His face was expressionless. He was more striking in person; his brows framing deep brown eyes with flecks of yellow. A few black locks of hair had escaped his hat and brushed against his forehead. I watched him lick his dry lips.

"No more phones," he said.

He was a real person, standing in the same physical space that I was in.

"No more phones," I said.

I reached out a hand.

"Hey," I said. "I'm Actual Tess."

He took my hand and gave it one brief shake. His palm was warm.

"Actual Daniel," he said.

"Nice to meet you."

I was staring, but I couldn't help it. I tried to look away, but it was impossible. I couldn't believe he was actually here.

"What, you weren't expecting a brown guy?" he said. "I sent you a picture."

I looked away.

"I wasn't expecting anyone," I said.

We were by the open door of the club, and there was a change in the music. All day there had been a steady blast of horns and rolling pianos. Raucous old music that brought raucous old women to the stage. Then suddenly, there came the soothing sound of Bobby Darin's voice. A song I remembered from the Oldies station my grandma used to listen to. *Beyond the Sea.* All of the dancers started to gather on the stage.

"How did you find me?" I asked Daniel.

I still wasn't sure that he was standing next to me. But I could smell the soap on his skin.

"Magic," he said.

I looked at him.

"I called your dad. His number's online."

I turned back to the stage and listened to the song.

Somewhere beyond the sea. She's there watching for me.

The old dancers had been drinking most of the day, and now they were in various states of undress. Lilli was still in a corset from an earlier number. Candy was in a shimmery purple evening gown with a giant boa wrapped around her neck. Another woman, Maggie L'amour, was topless, her drooping breasts covered only by pasties the size of silver dollars.

"This is what you've been doing since you dropped out?" Daniel asked.

"Pretty much," I said.

Mamie's friends wobbled and kicked, arms around one another like a last-ditch chorus line. And as the song picked up steam, moving into that revved up orchestra part, Candy led them in Mamie Lee's trademark shimmy. One at a time, they lay down on the floor and raised their legs straight up in a full-body quake until it was all wiggly thighs and Bobby Darin singing:

Happy we'll be beyond the sea. Never again I'll go sailing.

"Is this actually happening?" asked Daniel.

I could feel him watching me out of the corner of his eye, shyly taking in a face he'd only seen in pictures. His proximity was unnerving, but my heartbeat would not slow down. I had no idea where things were supposed to go from here, so I just kept staring at the stage.

"I think so," I said.

It was the best I could do.

26

Then Daniel Torres was living in my house.

One day, he was a line of text, a disembodied voice, and the next day, he was sleeping on a couch in my living room.

Well, my dad's living room technically.

When I approached Dad after the funeral, to ask if Daniel could crash for a few days, he chose that very instant to pretend he was a real parent. Probably because Grace was standing there, he asked what he thought were real parent questions.

Did Daniel's guardians know he was here? (Yes.) Was he on drugs and planning to steal things from the house? (Probably not.) How did I know him? (Friend of a friend?) I could see him trying to think of additional, better questions, but in the moment, he seemed to draw a blank.

"Fine," he said. "But he sleeps on the sofa."

Daniel was fine with this, but he seemed to take it to mean that he was confined to the couch exclusively for the duration of his stay. So for the first few days, he sprawled out there with a laptop balancing on his small belly. Meanwhile, I flitted in and out of the room and made sorry attempts at conversation.

"How did you get here, anyway? You never said."

"The bus."

"Huh. The bus. Interesting."

"Yeah. There was a guy in the back guarding the toilet."

"No kidding."

"Totally. He wouldn't let anyone use it. He said it was an infringement on his rights."

"Hmm. Weird."

"Yeah."

And that was the best we could do.

We couldn't seem to get anything going. And I thought, on numerous occasions, that I'd made a terrible mistake by implying he should come here. I couldn't understand why things were so strained. After a couple days of relative silence, there were still no signs of improvement.

Then he showed up at my room.

At night.

Just a half hour before he appeared, I had gone down to the kitchen to get a snack. I'd heard him shuffling and twisting around on top of the cushions, taking small, frustrated breaths like a baby. I couldn't sleep either.

So I was awake when I heard the knock. I got up slowly. I assumed it was my father at first, come to ask me what the hell was going on with the odd teenage boy on our couch. Instead I found Daniel standing in the dark hallway, blinking at me.

I hadn't closed the shades, so there was enough moonlight in the room that we could see each other. He was wearing a baggy T-shirt, and his hair was matted against his forehead. He looked my way, and a sudden wave of self-consciousness broke over me. I was wearing ripped boxers and a tank top. Not exactly ready for prime time.

"Can I come in?" he asked in a whisper.

I considered this a minute. What were a gentleman caller's intentions when he showed up at your bedroom in the middle of the night? When I looked at his face, though, it didn't seem especially pervy. It seemed pensive and vulnerable. Also, I was pretty sure he wouldn't try anything sketchy with my father snoring down the hall. It probably wasn't the world's most cautious decision, but I let him in anyway.

He walked over to my bed and lay down with his eyes open. I waited about half a minute before I sat down on the other side, with a gulf of bed between us.

"I didn't think it would be this weird," he said finally.

I sighed. On the one hand it was a relief to hear him say it. On the other, it confirmed that things were weird for both of us.

"Maybe you don't want reality," I said. "Have you ever thought of that?"

"What do you mean?"

"How could the real me actually be as good as the hypothetical one? Maybe real me kind of sucks. I mean comparatively, of course. In most ways, I'm fucking awesome."

"Maybe," he said. "But real you doesn't suck."

I felt myself blushing in the dark.

"Should I go home?" he asked.

I didn't answer him because I honestly didn't know. And for the next minute, we just lay there on opposite sides of the bed like siblings in a hotel room.

"What do you do all day?" I asked eventually.

I wasn't looking at him, but I heard his head shift toward me.

"What?"

"On the couch?" I said. "When you're just sitting there with your computer. What do you do?"

He took a deep breath and rubbed his eyes.

"I can show you if you want," he said.

I nodded, and he immediately crawled out of bed and

disappeared back down the stairs. When he returned a couple of minutes later, he was carrying his laptop. He unfolded it, and the glowing screen lit up the room.

He opened his browser, and the homepage for Twitter appeared on the screen. I saw a familiar face in the little white Twitter frame. I sucked in a quick breath. It was Jonah. The same photo that he had used on Facebook for as long as I'd known (and not known) him.

It had been a while since I'd encountered the picture, and seeing it again was both gratifying and unnerving. It was an image that I used to love, one I kept myself away from these days for a reason. I looked at the most recent post on the feed and immediately felt a familiar sense of uneasiness. I turned to Daniel.

"This post is dated yesterday," I said.

He nodded.

The message said simply, **"So so many new planets!"** and then it linked to a recent article about new planets discovered by NASA's Keppler telescope. It looked like any other post from a Twitter user.

"I don't understand," I said. "Are you still pretending you're him?"

Daniel shook his head.

"I'm writing an app," he said. "It was our first assignment

in Computer Science. I started out making a game. But then I switched to this."

I tried not to meet Jonah's eyes in the photo.

"What is it?"

"It's called Post-Life. It allows you to stay active on social media after you're gone."

"Gone? As in . . ."

"As in dead," he said.

I looked at another of the Post-Life tweets.

"When I eat two chili dogs in a row, I usually hear the Braveheart sound track in my head."

"Who's writing these?" I asked.

"He is," he said. "I mean, kind of. The program surveys his entire online persona, filing away all his likes and dislikes, interests, and the speech patterns of his previous posts. Then it uses that information to generate new ones, which it sends to his friends."

I stared at the screen.

"How can he eat chili dogs if he's dead?"

Daniel pushed the hair back from his forehead.

"That's a bug I haven't quite worked out yet. It doesn't seem capable of distinguishing what a dead person can and can't do. An ideal version would just keep up his interests, you know, as if he were still alive."

"But he's not still alive."

"I know."

"And he didn't ask for this."

"I get that," he said.

There was a current of irritation in his voice for the first time.

"It's not done yet. And the service would be for people who actively subscribe. People who want to keep posting after life. Jonah's profile is just a test. For me."

He snapped his laptop shut, and the room went dark again.

"You think it's creepy, don't you?" he said.

"A little," I said.

He wiped his hand over his eyes.

"That seems to be the consensus," he said. "My teacher suggested I switch projects."

It was starting to rain lightly outside. More like a heavy mist than a storm.

"It's not the same," I said. "You can't keep him alive that way."

I watched as a small puddle slowly pooled against the windowsill.

"I have a problem," he said, "don't I?"

"No," I said.

He looked at me.

"You have a lot of problems."

He smiled, but only for an instant.

"I knew it was wrong to write to you as him," he said. "But I did it anyway. I wanted to keep him here."

He rolled over in bed so he was facing me. But we were still miles of bed apart.

"The starlings," I said.

"What about them?"

"Did you write that?"

He nodded.

"You wrote most of it, didn't you?"

"Yeah," he said. "Jonah was always better in person. At least when he was feeling good. I'm better online, I guess."

"Why did you stop?" I asked. "I didn't get any messages for a week or so before he actually died."

"After that day in the Public Gardens, I couldn't do it anymore. I think the truth of everything finally became clear to me. It wasn't a game. Jonah was a real person, and something was seriously wrong with him."

"Wait a minute," I interrupted.

"What?"

"You didn't write as him after the Public Gardens?"

"No," said Daniel.

"Are you sure?" I asked.

"Positive. Why?"

I sat up and opened Daniel's laptop. I signed into my e-mail. I should have known from the beginning, I thought. The problem was that Jonah didn't send too many e-mails by the end. It was rare. But, still, I should have known that this one wasn't Daniel's. I searched my messages and finally came upon it, alone in a sea of advertisements and Quaker school newsletters. I opened it and handed the computer to Daniel.

"Did you write this?" I asked him. "You have to be honest."

It read:

Hello, Tess Fowler,

The Internet tells me that the swans in the Public Gardens are named Romeo and Juliet, but that they're actually both female. People like a good love story on their terms, I guess. The swans there are mute swans, but that just means that they're "less vocal" than other kinds. Part of the way they communicate is through the fluttering of their wings in flight. I wish I could do that, don't you? I think I might like it better than talking. There are so many things I like better than talking.

It's odd that we never saw each other after that night in Iowa. I make so many plans, Tess Fowler. I see them so clearly in my head. The way they're supposed to go. You and me are in there, in one of the plans. We're walking along somewhere and it's really nice and casual and everything is so easy like it was when we were talking that night. It takes so much energy to make things easy for me. I have to go a thousand miles an hour to make it seem like I'm going ten.

The new plan, the one I'm making right now, is a retroactive plan. When we meet at the farmhouse, this time I wake up the next morning and I miss my ride to the airport in Des Moines. I miss my flight back to Boston. And instead I stay with you a couple days. I live in your dorm like a stowaway and you smuggle me food from the cafeteria. I only come out at night, and no one else knows but you. That's as far as I've gotten. But it seems like enough. Doesn't it, Tess?

Yours,

J.

I read the e-mail along with Daniel, and we stopped around the same time. Daniel looked at the desktop of his computer, a swirling galaxy of tiny white stars.

"I didn't write it," he said.

"Don't bullshit me," I said.

Instead of defending himself again, he just got quiet.

"I can't believe it," he said.

"What?"

"You got a good-bye."

At some point, we had moved closer together, maybe a foot apart. The drop in temperature had made the room chilly, but I didn't want to get up to shut the window.

"Is that what that is?"

Daniel frowned.

"I'm sorry," he said. "I know I shouldn't be jealous. It's petty. And I'm not proud."

"I get it," I said.

Then I sat up.

"Why don't you write yourself one," I said.

"What do you mean?" he said.

"What's the point of your stupid app otherwise?"

With my free hand, I clicked on the Twitter tab and Post-Life flashed back on the screen. Daniel looked at the screen in front of him. He slowly brought his hands to the keyboard. But he didn't type anything.

Looking at Jonah's picture, it was possible, for a moment, to pretend that he was really still out there somewhere, sending back updates from the unknown. But it didn't last long, that feeling of contact. It was just another trick, some digital sleight of hand. Daniel closed the laptop.

I expected him to get up and wander back downstairs. But he stayed where he was. And instead of moving farther away, he reached out his hand across the bed. I watched it there in the dark.

"I liked them," I said. "The things you wrote to me."

"Thanks," he said.

"It kind of complicates things, though."

"I know," he said.

"I thought they were coming from him."

"I know."

The rain outside was picking up, pinging against the screen. I moved my hand across the bed and set it on top of his.

27

The next morning I woke up in an empty bed.

The sun was up and Daniel was gone. And when I got up to pee, the whole house was quiet. I'll admit I panicked a little. Maybe, I thought, as I sat on the coldest toilet seat in human history, Daniel had gotten what he came for. We talked through a few things and that was all he needed. When I finished in the bathroom, I pulled on some pajama pants and went downstairs.

The couch was empty.

His computer was gone too.

I stepped through the quiet hallway of the house until I reached the kitchen and let out a deep breath.

There was Daniel at the kitchen table. A neglected bowl of cereal sat in front of him, along with a cup of my dad's burnt coffee. He was fully dressed, for once, in a pair of well-fitting jeans and a light blue button-down. His hair was combed in a loose part.

I hardly recognized him. He looked older and younger at the same time. He was looking over a bunch of documents and brochures. When I stepped closer, I saw they were materials from my dad's business.

"Your dad is a seriously weird guy," he said. "A science fiction dog funeral? Holy shit."

I wanted to tell him I was glad he was still here. What I said instead was: "Why are you dressed like a host at the Olive Garden?"

Daniel glanced down at his shirt. He smoothed it over his chest.

"I thought maybe we could go for a walk," he said. "I haven't seen anything but a strip club since I've been here."

I looked down at the pajama pants I'd been rocking for the last few days. They hung on me more than usual. I was getting skinny.

"You say that like it's a bad thing," I said.

I lingered by the table. Daniel watched me.

"Fine," I said. "Give me a minute."

Outside, the sun was high and the blue sky glowed like it was backlit. We squinted against the brightness after days inside. I had yet to retrace my steps to the lake since the day I followed my computer into the water, and I wasn't quite sure why I felt compelled to go there now. But, since my father was gone again, and my car was on E, there were few other attractions of note.

Daniel didn't seem to care. He shuffled along, a step behind me, pleased to be out of his self-imposed captivity. He rolled up the sleeves of his dress shirt and held his face up to the light, like he hadn't been in the sun in years.

"So why are you doing this?" he asked with his eyes closed.

I watched his face.

"Walking outside for no reason?" I said. "Because you asked me to."

He smiled.

"Helping your dad with his business."

"I'm his partner," I said.

I could hear the flatness in my own voice.

"I didn't ask what your role was. I asked *why* you're doing it?"

For a guy who didn't love talking, Daniel had a way of asking pointed questions.

"It helps just to do something," Daniel said, after a moment. "Is that it?"

He put his hands in his pockets.

"When I first came home from school after Jonah died,

I helped my dad repaint the garage. Then I did the whole house by myself, even though it looked fine. Every day, I climbed up the ladder and slapped on another coat. Dad was happy to provide the paint. The only thing he believes in is hard work, even if it's meaningless. It worked for a little while, though. I felt better. Maybe it was the endorphins. Or just having a sense of purpose. But I think mostly it was the distraction. . . ."

"—And that's what you think my life is right now," I interrupted. "The symbolic painting of a garage?"

My voice came out louder than I'd hoped, but Daniel didn't flinch.

"I don't know," he said. "That's why I'm asking."

We moved down the hill where the lake was quiet. There were no people on the path. And for a second, I felt that summer vacation sense of being alone and unsupervised in a daytime world. But I couldn't help thinking about my last time here.

"Tess?" he said.

"Sorry," I said. "Just zoning."

The calm lake appeared before us, divided in half. One side was dazzling white with reflected sunlight. The other half had the darkened aura of an abandoned bog.

"It's not a distraction," I said finally.

Daniel turned toward me.

"I am perfectly capable of distracting myself in other ways I'll have you know. For example: I enjoy books and recreational drugs and flirting with hot cowboys. So, I resent the implication that I would do this just to pass the time."

"Okay," he said. "Then why?"

"Well, because my dad needs help. That's one reason. He's not going to make it otherwise, and he's at a point in his life where he might not have many more chances. He's that much of a screwup."

"And?" said Daniel.

"And . . . I'm actually good at it," I said. "I can plan some-body's death party like a pro, and it feels good to not suck at something. I know you and Jonah were computer geniuses or whatever, but I've never really found my thing."

I looked at the water, clotted with patches of bright green algae.

"Is that it?" said Daniel.

I was heading toward the dock. I felt my heart rate in-crease as I grew closer and saw the sign cautioning against swimming.

"No," I said.

I imagined the feel of the slimy stuff on my bare arms,

the way it had adhered to me like a second skin when I made it to the surface. I closed my eyes. The sunlight flickered orange and yellow beneath my lids.

"I'm also doing it because I'm terrified," I said.

Daniel watched me a moment.

"Of what?" he said.

"Oh," I said. "Everything. But mostly my impermanence."

His eyes searched my face.

"Some people are comforted by that," I said. "Not me. I like existing. At least most of the time. I like having a body. I want to keep it. But someday I won't have it anymore. That's unsettling."

I looked at the chipped railing on the dock.

"And I'm scared of being buried underground where worms and bugs will digest my remains. I know I won't be conscious, but still. It doesn't sound pleasant. Does that sound pleasant to you? I'm scared of being burned into a pile of oxidized matter. I'm scared of rotting and decaying."

I was building up steam now.

"I'm scared that I don't matter, even a little bit, and that no one matters and nothing matters. I'm scared that it all matters and I'm fucking it up. I'm scared I'm living my short short life wrong in every possible way. I'm scared I've already made so many mistakes and I don't have enough time to fix them. I'm scared I won't die with the slightest amount of dignity, like on the toilet or watching Bravo. I'm scared no one will care when I do. I'm scared that the only person I ever loved wasn't real. I'm scared I will never get over him. And I'm scared I'm making the same mistake again."

Daniel took this in. He took a step toward me. I didn't want to look him in the eyes. I didn't know what might happen. So I walked past him out onto the dock.

"I live with all of this like lots of people do," I said, "and sometimes, I can keep it away. But when someone dies, there's a rupture in all that, right? And all those fears come pouring back in at once. Maybe a good funeral can help people face it."

I looked down into the muddy water, hoping maybe I could see my dearly departed laptop down there shimmering like a tiny futuristic shipwreck. But, of course, I could only see down a couple of feet.

"Maybe a good funeral can help people find enough order to keep going. At least it shows you that you're not alone. I wish I'd had that. But I didn't. So maybe I can help my dad give it to other people."

We were quiet for a moment after this. I looked deeper into the water.

"Tess," said Daniel.

He was by my side now.

"No more questions," I said. "That's all I have to say."

"Tess," he said again.

I turned to him. His brown eyes were wide.

"We need to plan a funeral," he said.

I just stood there a moment.

"For Jonah."

I pushed some blowing hair from my face.

"I think it might help us," he said.

I took another step toward him, and he put his arms around me. He held me tight. But it was okay. It felt good. I held him back. I don't know what it meant, but it was good just to cling for a moment. Like we were two parts of the same broken thing.

Me: **This is it, Jonah: the person you left me with.**

28

My dad came home later that evening, and I watched him stand out in the backyard, smoking a cigarette. He had supposedly quit a year ago, and so far the only times I'd seen him cheat were when he was stressed about something. But his face looked calm now in the orange light of dusk.

Which brought up another possibility. He'd probably been with Grace. He'd probably been with her all afternoon and all those other mornings when he disappeared with no excuse. And yes, he had probably *been* with Grace in the Biblical sense (insert very loud dry heave). When he walked inside, he held the scorched filter of his cigarette under the tap before tossing it in the trash.

"Your fly's unzipped," I said, and he nearly jumped out of his skin.

"Jesus, Tess!" he said. "What are you doing? Keeping watch?"

He looked down.

"My fly is fine."

"But you checked!" I said. "You checked because you're guilty! Guilty of having gross sex!"

He ran his hands through his hair.

"Don't say sex," he said.

"Sex," I said. "Screwing. Porking! Doing the nasty!"

He stood there in the light of the kitchen, looking mildly ashamed.

"Are you done?" he asked.

"Maybe," I said.

Then, before he could say anything else, I said: "If you want to spend your time with a traitorous floozy, that's your business. But I'm not happy about it."

"Floozy?" he said.

"She pretended to care about me to get in your pants. I think that's pretty obvious at this point."

"Tess," he said. "That's not true. She's a divorcee and we have a lot in common."

"Yeah, like you're both selfish assholes."

I could see him getting angrier. Hell hath no fury like a middle-aged man scolded.

"Hey!" he said. "Can you cut me some slack please?"

"You should print that on a T-shirt," I said.

He shook his head. His face was red.

"I thought she was going to be *my* friend," I said.

He walked over to the counter and got himself a glass of water. He took a long drink, and his anger seemed to fade a little.

"Huh," he said. "I thought you hated her."

"So did I," I said.

When he was done with his water, his shoulders slumped, and he just stood there looking at the sink full of dishes.

"Why are you even staying here if living with me is so miserable?" he said.

He sat down at the table. His question hung between us.

"That's a fair question," I said.

He waited for me to go on. And though it would have been easy to get up and walk away again, I found that my feet didn't want to do that. It was getting exhausting, all this evading.

"I lost someone," I said.

I took a breath. My father just watched.

"Somebody I think I loved."

I tried not to look at him.

"I feel stupid saying that because we barely knew each other as it turns out. But it's true. I loved him. Or maybe the idea of him. Anyway, he made things better for a while. And last year I needed that. For some reason, I couldn't do it myself."

My dad was looking me in the eyes now.

"Tess," he said.

"When I heard he was dead, I didn't know where to go. I couldn't be at school. I really just wanted to disappear for a while. But when it came time to leave, I just came here. And I think now it's because you don't pretend."

My father looked at me now.

"Pretend?"

"That death isn't part of things. I don't understand all the reasons you do what you do, maybe it's mostly for the money, but you deal with dying the best you can. I think maybe I knew that. So I came here. Even though we aren't that close anymore. Does that answer your question?"

He scratched his face, under his ear.

"God, Tess. I could have been more help if I had known what was going on," he said. "I wouldn't have . . ."

"I understand that," I said. "But I couldn't talk about it."

He closed his mouth. I expected more anger about my secret. He had probably been through hell trying to find out what was wrong with me. But now that I'd told him, he seemed relieved more than anything else. Finally, he reached out and slung an arm around me.

"I'm sorry," he said. "I love you and I'm sorry."

I leaned against his shoulder. He spoke softly:

"I thought maybe you were just here because you knew I didn't have the guts to kick you out," he said.

I spoke into his shoulder. "That might be another reason."

He smiled and pushed up the sleeves of his shirt.

"There is one thing you can do for me now," I said. "If you really want to help."

I leaned back against his arm.

"What's that?"

"Give me my share of the money from Mamie's funeral."

"Okay." He sighed. "There wasn't too much left. But why now?"

"I have to buy a plane ticket to Syracuse."

29

Daniel came downstairs and we explained everything as best we could.

We told my dad about Jonah, what he meant to both of us, and our desire to create a meaningful ceremony for him. I repeated what I'd told Daniel about the importance of funerals, and what I'd learned by working with him.

All the while, my father sat at the table, watching the two of us speak, sweeping his hair behind his ears and waiting for it to come untucked. His eyes shifted back and forth between us. Finally, when we were done with our pitch, he sat up straight and clasped his hands in front of him.

"Tess," he said, "I'm really glad you shared this with me. Thank you for doing that. But you do realize I would have to be a crazy person to let you travel across the country on your own, don't you?"

"No," I said. "Actually I don't realize that."

"She wouldn't be alone," said Daniel.

My dad silenced him with a long stare.

"You dropped out of high school," he said to me. "And it wasn't that long ago that you seemed on the verge of a breakdown. Also, you'd be going there with an older guy who I don't really even know. No offense, Daniel, but sleeping on my couch is one thing. Taking my daughter to New York is another."

"To be fair," I said, "I don't know Daniel that well, either. He's kind of a cipher."

"Not helping," said my father.

Daniel looked down at the floor.

"I understand your reasoning for all of this," Dad said. "And I think it's beautiful that you want to put together this kind of tribute. But, it sounds like you don't have a plan yet. You don't have an itinerary, or even a sense of what you want to do when you get to his hometown. Tess, how could I, in good conscience, send you on your way with a stranger and absolutely nothing in place? What the hell kind of father would I be?"

"The kind you've been the last two years," I said.

He didn't blink.

"That's not who I am anymore," he said.

I slumped against the wall of the kitchen and felt the old

wallpaper stick against my bare arms. I looked at Daniel, who seemed to be biting his lip.

"So where does that leave us?" I asked. "Everything is just shot down?"

My father looked surprised for a moment. He cocked his head.

"Of course not," he said. "I'm sorry. I guess I haven't been clear."

"What are you saying then?" asked Daniel.

A little smile passed across my father's lips.

"I'm saying, if you want to go, I'm going to have to come with you."

30

Over the next few days, we put together the very begin-
nings of a plan. The more we talked about it, the more we
agreed that we needed a better understanding of Jonah. If
we were going to plan something with significance, we had
to find out who he really was. Who he was when he wasn't
with us. So Daniel and I decided that we'd go to Jonah's
mom's house and see what she could tell us about him.

The problem, of course, was that she had been more than
a tad icy to Daniel when he first tried to reach out. She
hadn't allowed him to come to the small, non-funeral she
had, and she'd seemed reluctant to speak to him for very
long on the phone. If we called her again, Daniel seemed to
think, we could probably expect more of the same. So this
time, we decided, we would just show up on her doorstep
and hope she let us in.

We didn't share every detail with my dad.

What we told him was that we had an appointment with

Marian, Jonah's mother. That she was expecting us. And that we were just getting her blessing before we continued with our funeral plan. When we flew into the city of Syracuse, it was too early to check into our cheap hotel, so Dad found a spot in the bar while Daniel and I lugged our bags onto the bus to a neighborhood called Eastwood.

It was deemed "the village in the city," and as we entered it, we passed a strip of small businesses. A cigar shop, a dentist office, a restored movie theater with a terra-cotta facade. Jonah's mom's street was a little bland, but there were window boxes in most of the windows and well-groomed yards out front.

The house was a green split level with mint growing wild near the porch. Daniel and I walked up the long cement driveway and stood on the stoop for a moment. It was a Saturday, but the house looked dark inside.

"Maybe she works weekends," said Daniel.

"Maybe you're being a chickenshit," I said, and rang the doorbell.

There was no movement, and the house stayed just as dark.

"We should come back later," he said.

Ignoring him, I stepped down from the porch and walked along the side of the house. The homes were close together, and the sun barely found its way in between Jonah's house and the one next door. I shuffled over the rough cement until I reached a backyard.

It was half asphalt and half raised-bed garden. But the garden was completely overgrown with weeds. They were six, seven feet tall, standing guard around any vegetables that might be trapped inside. Also, the weeds, we noticed after a moment, were moving.

I unlocked the gate and stepped onto the asphalt. There was a pole for a basketball hoop on one side, but the rim was gone, leaving only the off-white backboard.

"Hello?" I said.

The weeds stopped moving for a moment. Then they rustled again and a hand emerged, clutching a dirty spade. It was followed by the body of a short, pretty woman in a purple bandanna. Even covered in dirt and sweat, the resemblance to Jonah was immediate. His tangled blond hair spilled out the back of her scarf, and when she looked directly at me it was with those same gray-blue eyes. She wiped her brow with a gardening glove but only smeared the dirt around further.

"I'm sorry, guys," she said. "I can't donate to the marching band this year."

We just stared at her.

"There have been some financial setbacks. I hope you kids have a good time on your trip, though."

She set down her small shovel, picked up a hoe, and turned back toward the forest of her garden without giving us a second look.

"Wait," said Daniel. "Miss. I'm . . ."

She turned around.

"What?" she said.

Daniel went silent. Marian's face was already pained, like the slightest human interaction was grating on her. I opened my mouth.

"We don't play in the marching band," I said. "In fact, I kind of hate marching bands. Does anyone really like them?"

Daniel gave me a get-to-the-point look.

"We're friends of Jonah's," I said. "We came to talk to you about him."

For a split second, her grimace disappeared, and I wasn't sure if she heard me right. But then she closed her eyes for a moment and vanished into the garden. I heard the hoe hit the ground and watched as a few of the giant weeds started to tremble.

"I'm not really in the mood for visitors today, guys," she said from inside. "I'll give you the web address for his foundation, though. Feel free to add a message to the message board. That would be really nice."

We both stood there for a second, staring into the weeds. They were brown stalks, dry looking, with little tufts of seeds at the top. They looked like they were left over from last year. I didn't want to leave this yard—and I knew I shouldn't—but I also wasn't sure what to do next. How aggressive could you really be with a grieving parent? We couldn't force her to talk about things if she didn't want to.

So, I was surprised when Daniel took a step forward. Instead of heading back through the gate the way I expected him to, he walked over to the garden and grabbed a pair of dirty leather gloves sitting in the yard. Then he put them on, flexed his hands, and just started yanking on one of the weeds.

I watched his muscles strain and, though it had never occurred to me before, he was strong for his size. He struggled with the weed for a minute, grunting a little. Then he gave it one last yank and up it came, roots heavy with dark soil. He broke the stalk in half and then moved on to the next one. Oddly enough, Marian didn't comment. She just kept working.

I watched for a minute or so, then started to help. With the two of us pulling, it was a little easier, and the second weed came up quickly. We moved on to a third. Then a fourth. Then, somehow, an hour passed without a single word being spoken. Marian worked in another part of the garden, tilling a patch of already weeded soil. Beneath some of the weeds we pulled up were some asparagus and what looked like the beginning of a zucchini plant.

As the sun got hotter, Daniel took off his T-shirt and put it over his head like a turban. I rolled up the sleeves of my V-neck until I could feel the heat on the tops of my shoulders. I'm not sure how long we were out there, but eventually when we had half the garden weeded, and the sun was too much to bear, Daniel and I sat down in a small patch of shade nearby.

Marian ducked into the house and reappeared with a pitcher of lemonade. It was full of ice, and sweating on the sides, and it was the best lemonade I've ever had. I chugged my first glass, but then tried to savor the second. We sat there and drank until the pitcher was empty. Then, finally, Marian spoke.

"This was our project together," she said. "Me and Jonah's."

Daniel and I both watched her.

"In high school he read this book about urban homesteading. The previous owners had a garden here. I was always too busy. But when Jonah got interested in something, he did not do it halfway. In weeks, he was trading seeds with people in the neighborhood. And guess who got conscripted to help? I did most of the planting actually. He made plans on his computer. This intricate blueprint with all the spacing mapped out."

She smiled, but her eyes seemed to strain against it.

"He stopped asking about it after I took him to college, though. That was the first sign, I think, that things were going wrong again. I kept the garden up at first, so it would look good when he got home, but then when he didn't seem to care, I let it go."

Her gaze lingered on the plot of dirt and scrubby vegetables. Then it gradually turned back to me. She studied my face for a moment.

"You're Tess," she said.

"How did you know that?"

"He told me about you. He didn't talk about girls very often, but he mentioned you. I knew it was you the moment you showed up. You're just as pretty as he said."

I felt my face turning red.

"And you're Daniel," she said.

He nodded.

"Where did you guys come from?" she asked.

"Minnesota," I said. "And outside Chicago."

If she thought anything of these places, she didn't say. She just took one last drink from her lemonade and swirled the ice around in her glass.

"And you came here because you're not sure you really knew him," she said. "Is that it?"

We were both silent.

"Well," she said. "You'll have to join the club."

She got up then to go inside. Daniel and I followed, and instead of shooing us away, she held the door open as we walked in. The inside of the house was cluttered, but not messy. There were books about fad diets and self-help stacked haphazardly on the shelves. It smelled like scented candles, something citrusy. It was all perfectly nice, but the living room felt spare to me for some reason. Eventually I realized it was because there were no family pictures.

"I don't know what to tell you," Marian said after a moment. "I'm not sure I knew him completely, either. I still couldn't tell you how things got so bad. He had the support of his family—his grandparents and me. He had counseling. He had medication. I made sure he saw someone at school. I checked in as much as I could. In the end, I think it was his own sense of shame more than anything else."

"Shame?" I said.

"He felt like he was deficient ever since he got his diagnosis of depression and anxiety in the eighth grade. He used to lie to his friends when he missed school. He'd say he had other conditions. Mono. Asthma. The flu. He wanted to be cured. Just having a good day or a good week wasn't enough. He was so hard on himself. Instead of learning to embrace who he was, he tried to be another person entirely. Someone flawless. If he was feeling less than perfect, he wouldn't let anyone see him. His friends at school only knew him as this smart, funny guy. They didn't know anything else."

"Neither did I," I said.

She nodded.

"It probably made him happy," said Marian. "To be his best self with you. To be who he wanted to be online like that."

She closed her eyes. And it seemed like she was about to cry. Daniel sensed this and I watched his body tighten up.

"What can you tell us about Sicily?" he asked quickly.

"What?" she said.

"I found this notebook. He wrote in it that he wanted to go to Italy. To Sicily specifically. It seemed like it was important to him. But maybe it was just a random thought or something. I don't know."

"Syracuse," Marian said.

"What?" Daniel said.

"I forgot all about that," she said. "Syracuse. That's where he wanted to go."

"You mean *here*?" I said.

"No," she said. "I mean Syracuse in Sicily. *Siracusa*."

I looked at Daniel. He was stone-faced.

"It's a city in Sicily. He saw it once on a travel show. I was in the other room, working on our taxes. He had been talking to me from the living room about computer science classes he wanted to take in college. Then he just went silent. I asked him a couple of questions that went unanswered until finally I got up from the table and came into the room and he was just staring at the TV."

"Look," he said. "Another Syracuse."

"And we both watched the host walk through the beautiful ancient streets of the city's historic district. Jonah looked mesmerized. At one point he said something so quiet I almost didn't hear him."

"What did you say, sweetie?" I asked.

"That's where I live," he said.

"That's where you *want* to live?" I asked.

"No," he said. "That's where I live right now. The other me."

"What other you?" I asked him.

"The . . . one who's not depressed. He lives in the other Syracuse. And he walks those streets in that bright sun everyday. I'm sure of it."

"I told him there was no *other* him. That he was the perfect version. But I could see that he wasn't listening. That he had kind of stuck on this idea. That there was this alternate city with an alternate him in it. I never heard him talk about going there, though."

"It was a place he wanted to go when he felt better," said Daniel. "That's how it seemed."

Now Marian really did start crying, and it was one of the hardest things I've ever had to watch. I got up after a minute or two and got her a glass of water. She drank half of it and smiled at me through her tears.

"Where are you two staying tonight?" she asked.

"At a hotel," I said. "Near the university."

"We should probably get back," Daniel said.

She took another drink of water and then put a hand on my arm.

"I'd like you to stay here," she said. "Just for a night. Would you do that?"

31

So we did. We were a little uneasy about the whole thing, but we agreed because how could we really say no? Marian made us spaghetti with some of the basil we'd uncovered in the garden. We ate. We drank tumblers of diet soda. She pulled some old Popsicles out of the freezer, and we politely licked the frost off of them. She didn't mention Jonah again. Instead, she asked us mom questions about ourselves.

I lied and said I was still at Quaker school, and Daniel talked about college. It didn't seem right to tell her that our lives had been so shaken by the death of her son. That we had both dropped out of life in different ways because of it. Maybe a part of her wanted to hear that life couldn't go on without him, but I was too afraid it would compound her pain.

At some point, I called my confused father and told him where we were staying. Then it was time for bed. This time around I was the one on the couch. Which meant Daniel was in Jonah's room. All night Marian hadn't once invited us in there, but then when the time came to sleep, she just casually told Daniel it was his room for the night. I could tell he was a little freaked out, but he didn't let on to Marian. He just disappeared down the hall and shut the door.

I got a text message only a minute or two later.

Not sure how to feel about this . . .

I wrote back quickly:

What's it like in there?

A few seconds passed.

It's like being inside his head as a child, I guess. It still feels like a boy's room.

Are you sleeping in his bed?

On the floor.

Which made sense to me. The bed might be too much, even for me.

What do you see?

I thought about telling him to take pictures, to do a panoramic shot of the whole room, but I resisted and left my message as it was.

You want me to list things?

Exactly.

I typed again:

Please. List things.

There was a significant pause. I assumed it was because he was writing a longer text, taking his time to catalog every single item in the room. But when his next text came back, it was short. And all it said was:

Things I'm seeing without you:

I shut my eyes for a second. I had thought, stupidly, that I only ever played this game with Jonah. Never with Daniel. But of course, he knew about it, too.

Model airplanes.

Those were the first words. They stuck there, alone for a moment in their own text bubble. But they were soon followed by others.

I don't know my planes well enough.
My dad would know. They look like
they're from one of the World Wars.
They're hanging from dental floss over
the bed. Maybe in some kind of dog-
fight. All I can see are the undersides.

I watched my phone and waited for the next update.

Quotes on the wall. Written in cursive.
Probably his handwriting. I remember seeing
it on Post-its around our dorm room. It's too
dim to read them now. But here's one over
his desk by the light. "If you tell the truth,
you don't have to remember anything."

I interrupted for just a moment.

Mark Twain.

Daniel kept going.

Trophies and certificates from Quiz
Bowl competitions. There's a shelf
built especially for them. Most of them
first place. State competitions. Some
individual. He won a lot. More than I've
ever won for anything. He's in the paper,
too, shaking the governor's hand.

A pause and then:

High school dance photos. He looks so young.
He has braces in most of them. Red and blue
rubber bands. The girls look nice. Sweet. He's in
one by himself, early on, pretending to hold an
invisible date. He has a hand on the small of her
back, and another on her waist. He has a serious
look on his face. Like he's in love. The dance is
called the Spring Fling.

Daniel was typing fast now, the messages popping up one after the other, and I was hesitant to interrupt him again. I wanted to know about every detail of the room. I wanted him to tell me every last thing he saw. But I slipped in one response. I couldn't help it.

That's me.

This seemed to throw off his rhythm. It put a halt to his listing.

Who?

The missing girl
in the picture.

I wrote again:

The one who isn't there.

Now his rhythm was definitely off. The streaming sentences of description came to a stop, and the screen remained unchanged. I wondered for a moment if I'd shut it down completely, but another reply came eventually.

I wish sometimes I could
pretend again.

Pretend what?

That I'm him. It was easier that way.
Easier than being me. And maybe
you'd be happier.

It's not the right kind
of happiness.

A few seconds passed. Then he responded:

I was hoping I'd know him completely
after coming here. That I would get
all the answers and it would all finally
make sense.

He wrote again:

I thought I would solve the mystery.
But there aren't any real clues here.
Just airplanes.

I leaned my head against the armrest of the couch. It was hard against my neck. I wrote without thinking much.

I just let the words unfold from my fingertips.

We're not going to plan a
funeral here, are we?

No.

I could feel my palms starting to sweat.

I have an idea that I can't
get out of my head. I don't
even want to say it.

His response came quickly.

Say it.

You already know what it is,
don't you?

I think I do.

But it's crazy, right? It's not
going to happen.

Why not?

There was a pause as I collected my thoughts for a moment.

> If we're on the same page
> here, and I'm not sure that
> we are, I don't know what
> to tell my dad. How will
> we convince him?

It seemed like a long time before his next message arrived, but it was probably only twenty seconds or so.

I don't know. Maybe we shouldn't.

My head was starting to feel light.

> We just leave him?

We just leave him.

I could feel my heart beating so fast in my chest.

> Do you have a passport?

This time his response was fast. And after it arrived, I had a hard time getting to sleep. Instead I just sat there looking at it, trying to decide what to do. It read:

Yes. And I brought yours.

32

As it turned out, Daniel had never stopped thinking about Sicily. Ever since he saw that note on Jonah's desk, it had been coming back to him again and again. And now that he'd heard Marian's explanation, going there seemed like the only choice left. I wasn't so sure. It seemed right in some ways, but extreme in others. What exactly would we do or find there? But after rattling off my worries for a half hour the next morning, Daniel silenced them with two sentences.

"It's the life he should have had," he said. "I think we should see it."

An hour later, I used my emergency credit card to book two tickets to Palermo. The tickets were almost three thousand dollars, which is more than I have ever spent on anything in my life. The parental fallout from this was going to be swift and harsh. I would likely be paying these off for the next five years. But when the "buy" button came up on my phone, I tapped it with a shaky finger and before I could blink, the transaction was complete.

Then I took a deep breath and texted my dad. I told him that I needed another half day to talk to Marian. And then, while he thought I was soul-searching with a grieving mother, Daniel and I took a cab to the airport and boarded the first leg of our international flight. Just like that.

I expected to get stopped. I expected security to flag me and send me home. But I was a well-dressed middle-class girl with someone who appeared to be my boyfriend, and nobody cared. Daniel was a little more worried, so we worked out a story beforehand. Anyone who asked, we told the same thing. We were college freshmen, going to Italy for a summer language immersion program. *Ciao, bella!*

I didn't text my dad again until we got to our first stopover in Toronto. By then he must have been worried for a few hours. I wrote:

> I am completely aware that you will never forgive me for this. And I know Mom will probably try to have you arrested. But this was the only way I could imagine to release myself from everything I've been feeling.
> I had to do it without you. I'll call you from Sicily.

It wasn't until I was safely on my third flight that I remembered the small container I had smuggled on board in my carry-on. It was wedged between the last of my clean underwear and some granola bars, but it was still there: a small plastic bowl with a powdered version of Jonah inside. The ashes were grayish white with tiny hard bits here and there.

Our plan hadn't exactly come as a surprise to Marian that morning, but she didn't say anything for a few seconds after we told her. Eventually though, she got off the couch and brought us a small scoop of Jonah's ashes. She put them in a Tupperware container with a blue lid.

After she handed them to me, I held them tight, unwilling to stuff them in the duffel bag Daniel had brought with him. She didn't say anything right away. She just walked us outside and back down the sidewalk. Her eyes were cocooned in the eye makeup she'd never washed off from the night before. Her smile when she spoke was brief and tight-lipped. All she said was: "Say hi if you see him."

Then she gave us both a long hug and disappeared back into her dark house.

Now I was all alone in an aisle seat, 39,000 feet above the earth, with the mineral fragments of a boy I once loved in my hands. Daniel was up ten rows with a sleeping mask on.

We couldn't get seats together. I had planned on dozing my way across the Atlantic—this final leg of our flight was at night—but, of course, I couldn't sleep.

I tried reading an in-flight magazine, but the lives of the people inside were so full of enthusiasm and confidence that I couldn't even distract myself by pretending to be them. And the more I sat there, the more the doubts started to creep back in. I took a few deep breaths and let them out through my nose. Eventually, the woman in the seat next to me leaned over and extended a pack of gum.

"The air pressure bothers me, too," she said with a smile.

I pulled out a stick. It was easier than turning it down. The woman was about my mom's age, with dyed blond hair and light gray roots. And she was clearly in the mood to chat.

"What brings you to Italy?" she asked.

"A funeral," I said, and turned away.

"Oh," said the woman. "I'm sorry. What a shame."

I put the piece of gum in my mouth; the artificial sweetener coated my tongue.

"Why is it a shame?" I asked.

"Oh," said the woman again, blushing a little. "I don't know. I guess I just meant it's such a beautiful country. I wouldn't want to visit it for something like that. But I'm sorry for your loss. I didn't mean to . . ."

"Don't worry," I said. "It's okay."

I saw my opportunity to disengage if I wanted to. Instead, I spoke again.

"I actually agree with you in a way," I said. "In fact, if you want to know the truth, the dead person isn't even from Italy. We're bringing him in ash form. I have him right here."

She looked at the Tupperware bowl and inched slightly closer to the window.

"This is just part of him," I said. "But, as I was saying, if you look at the situation in one way, the whole thing is kind of a giant waste. He's a pile of dust. He doesn't care where he is. And he never even went to Sicily while he was alive. Why would he want to come here now when he can't actually experience it?"

The woman's face was locked in a tight-lipped grimace.

"And believe me, this is not the way I wanted to see Italy. I thought I'd be going to Venice with a sexy Philosophy major to drink Bellinis and make out on a gondola. I didn't think I'd be coming here to plan something for a dead person. This was not the way I had it drawn up, I'll tell you that much."

The woman was miraculously still making eye contact with me. She was, however, holding tight to her armrest.

"But then, I'm also thinking: maybe this is the right way to see it. Because, maybe the one good thing about the dead, if there is anything good about them—which there totally might not be—is that they remind us that it's actually going to happen. Any old time."

I motioned toward the small window to my right.

"And meanwhile, there's all this stuff. Crazy, sublime stuff. And we're blind to it all the time. Or, at least, I am. I don't know about you—I won't speak for you—but I don't notice anything. I've been walking around like a goddamn zombie for months. I don't even hear the birds. I don't hear them! They make such beautiful little chirps, and I don't care. I don't care about their chirps. I don't care if they find mates. But I really want to try to care. I want to try to pay attention to the sublime, amazing stuff. Do you get what I'm saying?"

I took a breath and brought my seat back up to its original position. A passenger from the row in front made eye contact with me through the crack between seats but quickly looked away. I closed my eyes. The woman next to me was quiet. After a moment I leaned over to her and said, "Thanks for the gum."

Then I looked down the row at Daniel. I wondered if he'd heard any of the conversation, but it was probably too noisy to hear much. I only saw a sliver of his face through the seats. He was leaning against the window like a child. I wondered suddenly if he had a bad association with air travel because of his dad's work. I hadn't asked him anything about himself in days.

Suddenly, I had a profound urge to have him sitting next to me. Just sitting there, talking about everything in his soft, deliberate voice. Also, I liked holding hands during landings, and he had humored me on the other two flights. I had reached for him and he was there. He didn't even look at me in those moments. He just grasped my hand and closed his eyes. And, both times, it had eased the anxiety.

But the woman next to me probably wasn't going to change seats. Especially now. I'd be lucky if she hadn't reported me to a flight attendant. So, for the moment, I just sat there looking at the side of his face, rows away, wondering if he was the last person on earth who didn't think I was completely out of my mind.

33

Now seems like a good time to admit that I've never really been out of the country. I was in Canada once when I was a kid, but Canada doesn't really count. It's Minnesota with Mounties. The only reason I had a passport at all was because my mom was always threatening to take me away on spiritual journeys to lands unknown. Anyway, this is all just to say that I was not really prepared for the city of Palermo when we arrived.

It was midday when we got there, and the traffic was a total cluster: one huge game of chicken between hundreds of Fiats and motos, all carrying an improbable number of humans. In the cab to this intersection called the Quattro Canti, I looked out my window and saw an entire family riding on a single scooter. Seriously: four people. One scooter.

The toddler was first, just kind of perched on his father's lap. Dad was next, one hand on the throttle, lit cigarette dangling from his lip. Behind him was the mother, holding on to her husband like she was giving him the Heimlich. And behind her, barely on the seat at all was a sullen teenage boy. All of them were tan. None of them wore helmets. And just when I was about to point this sight out to Daniel, the family took off at an inhuman speed, balancing like acrobats.

Daniel was passed out anyway. He didn't do well on planes, he told me, and I'm pretty sure he downed half a package of Dramamine before we left. While he slept with his mouth open, I tried to soak up the street life on the ride to the hotel. The sun-whitened Baroque churches and smoking shop owners, the flocks of kids my age with plumed haircuts typing frantically on their phones. I only caught glimpses as the taxi pinballed its way through the city.

Finally, we arrived at the Centrale Palace Hotel, which was way too nice for us. We stumbled into the frescoed lobby and stood beneath a dazzling antique chandelier. Daniel had booked the hotel and the place was completely bonkers, a former eighteenth-century aristocratic residence remodeled into a hotel for travelers. In other words: the kind of place I never stayed, and probably would never stay again.

"How the hell can you afford this place?" I asked.

"I paint houses in the summer," he said.

He looked up at the chandelier.

"This room was like . . . ten houses."

Daniel walked to the desk and rang the bell.

A clerk strolled across the marble floor dressed in a powder-white linen suit. His neck and face were covered in expertly groomed stubble.

"Benvenuti a Sicilia!" he said. "You are on your honeymoon, yes? You said this in your reservation. But, *regazzi,* you are so young!"

I was still staring at his suit. Fortunately, Daniel came to life beside me.

"Yes," he said. "*Si.* We're on our honeymoon. We're young, but we're super Christian. *Bambino Gesú!* We love that guy! So that's why we're so young and everything. We saved ourselves for the Lord. Sexually."

I think Daniel was still high on Dramamine. The clerk just smiled, his blue eyes sparkling in the light of the chandelier.

"Bene," he said. *"Bambino Gesú. Bene."*

He winked. Then he took our passports and typed our information into a computer. All the while he kept sneaking glances at us. Either he was stealing our identities or picturing us having sex. I couldn't decide which I preferred. Then, abruptly, he began walking toward a minuscule elevator, speaking over his shoulder.

"*Andiamo*," he said. "I show for you now, the room, *ragazzi*. Follow me. Follow me."

We went up a few floors and the room he showed was beautiful, but small, with two toilets. My glance volleyed between the two.

"That one is the bidet," said Daniel, reading my mind.

I turned it on and it shot out a stream of boiling water.

"How do you know all of this?" I asked.

He shrugged and sat down on the bed.

"My dad used to be in the Air Force. We traveled a lot. I've seen my share of toilets."

"I see," I said. "A real toilet connoisseur."

"Something like that."

I nodded. And then everything got sort of quiet. It took me a moment to realize it was because we were in a hotel room together. Alone. In another country.

Did I mention alone?

Up until now, most of our interactions had been chaperoned in some way. Now there was no one in the room but us. So, I stayed in the bathroom for a minute, switching the bidet on and off, pretending to be fascinated by it. Finally,

I walked out and just looked at Daniel on the bed. His face was really tired. His eyes were slits. His dark hair was sticking up in the front.

"What are we really doing here?" I said.

He opened his eyes a little more.

"We're creating something for Jonah," he said.

"Is that true?"

I walked over and sat at the foot of the bed. There were fresh flowers in the room and the smell was overpowering.

"I don't know anything about this place," I continued. "I don't know what he would want here. And I don't know if I'm really here for him."

I slumped over on my side and watched the gauzy curtains ripple in a breeze.

"So, why are you here then?" said Daniel.

His voice was quiet.

"I don't know yet," I said. "Maybe it's just to escape. Maybe it's . . . for other reasons."

He leaned back against his pillow and closed his eyes.

"Okay," he said. "Say that's true. Is it so bad?"

"The whole idea was to plan a funeral for Jonah."

"So what?" he said.

I looked at him through narrowed eyes.

"What do you mean 'so what'?"

"I mean there's no protocol for this, Tess. We're on our own with our grief. But at least we're not pretending that nothing happened. At least we're trying something. Maybe we can forgive ourselves a little bit."

I stayed where I was.

"If you wanted to get me in a hotel room," I said, "we didn't need to fly all the way to Italy. There's probably dirty motels in New York."

"That's not fair," he said.

He sounded genuinely hurt, but I didn't turn around to see his face. We were quiet then for a few minutes. Outside, I could still hear the traffic in the street. The staccato honk of the horns. I heard Daniel breathing heavily and I thought maybe he had gone to sleep. But, then he spoke up again.

"You don't really think he's watching us, do you?" he said.

He paused a moment.

"I mean, you don't believe . . ."

"I don't think so," I said. "It's hard, but I don't think so. I thought he was still alive on the Internet for a while, but it just turned out to be some creep who was stalking me."

Daniel sighed.

"Why would anyone who's dead spend their time

watching the living?" he said. "That's what I want to know. If there's an afterlife, there have to be more interesting things to do."

"Like what?" I said.

"I don't know," he said. "Flying. Being out of your corporeal body. Living outside of time. Any of that would beat the TV station of my life. I can tell you that much."

"Mine too, I guess," I said. "Except when I'm naked."

He didn't say anything to that. I raised my body off the mattress and crawled up to the top of the bed and settled into a spot next to him. We lay still for a minute, only inches apart. I felt like I could feel every ounce of blood pulsing through my body.

"Put your arm around me," I said.

He put his arm around me.

"No," I said. "Like this."

I moved it over my hip and across my waist. He kept it there.

"Look," I said. "I didn't really mean what I said before. About the hotel. But I just want you to know, I have to be here for Jonah. It's the only thing that's holding things together right now."

I rested my hand on his chest.

"I understand," he said.

I blinked. The jet lag was finally kicking in, and I found I could barely keep my eyes open.

"Some honeymoon, huh?" I said.

He let out a long breath.

"I don't have any others to compare it to," he said. "Maybe it's perfect."

And with that, we both closed our eyes.

34

The next morning, we grabbed our small bags and boarded a tour bus and took off through the heart of Sicily. The bus was big enough for fifty, but there were only five of us. Me and Daniel and some random guys on a TV film crew from the States. There was a hefty dude named Paul, who had the largest, thickest black glasses I have ever seen, and another slightly less hefty man named Archie, who had tattoo sleeves and a fanny pack.

The film guys were camped out at the back of the bus, surrounded by black cases of equipment, passing a tablet Scrabble game back and forth without speaking. Finally, there was our driver, a white-haired Sicilian who only answered to Capo. Within the first ten minutes of the ride, he shouted a word that sounded like "catso" over and over again. I asked Daniel to look it up on his phone and we found out it meant "dick."

I kept thinking that I should have felt calmer—I was on

a bus, finally heading to Siracusa, a place with real meaning for Jonah. Instead my nerves were fraying one at a time. The problem was that there were still so many loose ends. We didn't have a plan yet for the ceremony. We didn't even know where we were staying. And I had yet to turn on my phone to see the barrage of messages from my father and others.

As soon as this bus came to a halt I was going to have to create something meaningful with nothing but a tiny container of ashes. I tried to do some deep breathing, pulling the stale air of the bus through my nostrils. After a few breaths, I felt a hand on my shoulder. It was Daniel, reaching over from the seat next to me.

"Look," he said, motioning out the window. "It's so green."

He still looked a little out of it from the Dramamine. His hair was messy, and his eyes were glazed. But I followed his pointer finger to the landscape rushing past the bus, and it was, without a doubt, green.

I didn't know much about Sicily, but I had imagined it sunbaked and dusty, beige cities edged by rinds of twinkling turquoise water. But this was the height of spring, and the land outside was an unending sweep of green hills leading to the foot of olive-colored mountains. The only break in the wall of green was the occasional citrus grove, bursting with fat lemons.

I felt a momentary calm come over me. How could anything bad happen in a place that looked like this? I wasn't the only one moved. When I turned to look at the back of the bus, I saw Paul aiming a state-of-the-art digital camcorder out the window, trying to capture what I'd just been admiring. He was showing a sizable amount of plumber's crack, and Archie was behind him, helping him hold the camera steady.

An hour passed like this. A series of gorgeous landscapes and hairpin turns down narrow roads. After a while, I started to take the scenery for granted. My eyes glazed over and I let the green of the land and the blue of the sky blur together. I had been dozing off and on for about fifteen minutes when the bus took a sharp turn around a bend and I opened my eyes wider. I caught sight of something in the distance. Up a steep grassy hill, split in half by a row of cypress trees, was a tight cluster of little houses. A small walled-in town.

The layout was a perfect rectangle. I had never seen a town so compact and perfectly planned. But that's because it wasn't a town at all. As we got closer, I could see that the small-scale houses were made of stone. And they weren't houses. They were mausoleums.

"Stop!" I said. "Stop the bus, please!"

At the sound of my voice, Capo stomped on the brakes, and the bus jerked to a skidding halt on the winding road. I held on to Daniel's arm and braced myself. Behind me, Paul slammed into a seat back, somehow keeping hold of the camera as his black-rimmed glasses launched from his face.

"What in the hell was that?" he said.

I met each of the men's eyes individually. I cleared my throat.

"I apologize for the abrupt stop, guys, but . . . um . . . I'd like to step outside just for a moment to see something. Thanks. *Grazie.* Thanks."

I motioned to a stunned-looking Daniel, and he followed me off the bus and onto the gravel-strewn road. There were no other cars and the air was as fresh as I'd ever breathed. I crossed the road and began to walk up the hill toward the walled cemetery-town before me. Daniel was a step or two behind.

The others were slow to leave the bus but, by and by, I heard the sounds of their voices, too. Eventually, I reached an open gate and stepped inside to find a series of streets, complete with tiled signs, lined by one-story crypts, each bearing a small black-and-white photo of the entombed.

I started walking down a street named Viale San

Giovanni, and as I got farther toward the center, the tombs became more ornate. Some of them were more like churches than homes, their facades swirling with carvings of angels. But of course there were churches; I was in a city for the dead.

It should have been spooky. We were the only ones in the cemetery, walking the streets of a literal ghost town. But, when I approached one particular mausoleum with a small dome on top, I looked at the two images of a married couple, grinning in black-and-white, and I felt comforted somehow. At least they were together.

I turned around to see Daniel watching me. I wanted to say something to him, but I didn't know what. Then I heard a loud, unintelligible sentence from behind me.

"What was that?" I asked.

Capo took a step forward.

"*Un terremoto,*" he said.

He paused a second, squinting as if he were searching for something on the horizon. Then he shook his hands. "The earth . . . quakes!" he said. "*Capito?*"

"There was an earthquake here?" Daniel asked.

"*Sì,*" said Capo. "*Un terribile terremoto.*"

I noticed then that Paul was filming this, too. Capo walked up and stood directly in front of the camera, as if he had just been waiting for this moment to host his own television show.

"The whole *città* . . . *tutto* destroy. *Abbandonato!*"

I looked again at the little crypt homes.

"These are the victims?"

Capo seemed to understand. He nodded and gestured toward the crypts. I reached out and touched a wall. It was rough and chalky against my palm.

"So, this is the only town left?" I said.

Everyone was quiet.

I looked at the nearby tombs. Most of the pictures portrayed the victims in their youth. I didn't know if this was because they'd actually died young or because these were the only photos the bereaved could find.

But each face seemed not much older than Jonah's.

"It must be a relief," I said.

Daniel squinted at me.

"How do you mean?" he said.

"To the families. Just to know the dead are not alone," I said. "They have a whole town. They have one another."

Capo crossed himself before he walked back to the bus and started it up again. Paul and Archie put their equipment down and took their seats. We rode for the next few hours in silence, and finally, in the early afternoon, the bus pulled up to the outskirts of Siracusa, unable to go farther due to the narrow roads.

Daniel and I stepped out with our bags. The film crew stood surrounded by dollys, mics, and lens shades, like castaways with no tools useful for survival. I walked up to them.

"What are you guys filming, anyway?" I said.

They looked at each other. Then Paul stepped forward.

"We don't really know," he said. "Some kind of Italian nature show. But we haven't heard from the client in days. Instructions have been a little loose."

I looked them over. The beginning of an idea was coming to me.

"How would you gentlemen like some side work?" I said.

35

Bringing on a film crew for no specific reason was my first mistake. Turning my phone back on was my second. As we crossed the Ponte Umbertino, a bridge into the historic quarter of Siracusa, Daniel was asking a lot of questions about the first of these decisions.

"What are we going to use those guys for?" he said. "I thought this was just for us. Seriously, Tess, why did you ask them? I don't understand it."

Meanwhile, I watched the message app on my phone explode with angry texts. I opened it up and glanced at the feed. I saw phrases like "calling the embassy" and "have him arrested." And farther toward the top. "I'm afraid for you, Tess. I'm not sure you're thinking clearly." I tuned back to Daniel, who was chattering away beside me.

". . . just don't want to do anything over the top like your dad does. This isn't some customer we're trying to dupe;

Jonah was our friend. It just doesn't feel right to do some kind of gimmicky thing—"

"Excuse me," I said.

"What?" he said.

Below us, on the reflective water of an inlet, some tied-up kayaks drifted into one another.

"What the hell did you just say?"

Daniel took his sunglasses off to wipe them on his shirt. His eyes squinted in the sun. He shifted his duffel bag to his other shoulder and avoided looking at me.

"I'm just saying I don't know why you asked that film crew—"

"After that."

He sighed.

"Look, Tess. I like your dad. He's cool and weird, but his ideas are kind of ridiculous. You can see that, right? I just don't want Jonah's thing to be a joke like that."

My throat was tightening. I felt my fist clench at my side.

"Mamie's funeral was a joke to you?"

"The one with the *strippers*?"

"Yes," I said. "The one where a woman who had been censored by her husband got a final celebration with her old friends. Doing what they loved. That was a gimmick?"

"Tess," he said. "C'mon. You know what I mean."

But in that moment, I didn't. So, I just started walking.

"Wait a minute!" he said. "Where are you going?"

He started to jog to catch up. I turned around and stopped him in his tracks.

"I don't want to see you right now," I said. "Go manipulate someone else into hanging out with you."

His shoulders dropped and he looked down at the cobblestones. He clearly wanted to be comforted, but I couldn't do that right now. I had no comfort to give. So, I just kept walking into Ortygia, the historical center of Siracusa. I took deep breaths and tried to forget everything except being here in this present moment.

Everything on the island was quiet. Everyone was taking their afternoon naps. All of the little businesses had closed their metal shutters, and the outdoor displays of Limoncello and foldable chalkboards with seafood specials were safely stored inside.

There were only a few wandering tourists. It was a beautiful place, though. Maybe the prettiest place I'd ever been. A Mediterranean palette of two-story buildings in reds, pinks, beiges, and yellows. The stone facades were chalky like coral, and the balconies were crowded with succulents, spilling over the metal railings. If I squinted my eyes, I could almost pretend I was underwater. No wonder Jonah romanticized this place.

I kept walking until I hit my first major landmark. The Temple of Athena. It was absolutely massive, bright white and ornate. A sign nearby said it was from the fifth century BC. And it gave way to the smoothest, cleanest public space I had ever been in. I almost felt like I should wipe my feet before stepping onto the time-smoothed stone beneath me.

The sun reflected off the white stone and seemed to create a burst of light around everything. I moved toward a bench on the far end of the piazza. I knew as I approached it that I was going to lose it once I sat down. It was all too much. All of this. I needed to cry or lie down or both.

I got within a foot of the bench when I saw him.

He looked self-possessed, sitting there by himself, sipping an espresso beneath a sign that read "Caffe Minerva." It wasn't an exact match, but it was close. He had the tangled blond hair and the glasses. And his body was lanky and lean in dark jeans and a crisp white T-shirt. The café must have just closed, but still, he sat there alone.

The other Jonah.

Right when I was about to take a seat nearby, he finished his coffee and dropped some Euro coins on the table. Then he got up and began to walk away. I wanted to call out to him, but what would I say? "Hey, you! Stranger! You're my dead Internet boyfriend's doppelganger!"

So, instead, I followed him across the piazza to the opening of a narrow cobblestone street. I realized on some level that what I was doing was not rational. The world was telling me to pull myself together and stop acting ridiculous, and I was calmly saying: *No, world. Sorry. I will keep at it.*

I followed him past more of the colorful two-stories. And as we got closer to the water, I could hear waves crashing against a seawall. A dusty van advertising BOAT TRIPS TO SEA CAVE! drove by with a small dog in the passenger seat. When we left the narrow road, there were thick palm trees growing crooked along a waterfront walkway. I watched as Other Jonah climbed a set of stairs up to a long lookout over the ocean. I went up the stairs about twenty feet behind him.

Nobody was at the top of the stone platform except for a few tourists spooning icy slushes in the sun. I couldn't tell if he knew I was there. I watched him without speaking, and he didn't turn around. We looked out at the same seascape: a foamy swathe of sky-blue water engulfing the rocks of a rugged beach. The waves lapped against a faded pink embankment.

But it was the ground that caught my attention.

LUCA + MARA, I saw directly beneath my feet. The names were written in red spray paint on the light stone, followed by *TI AMO*. I took a step to the side and saw another piece of graffiti. GIO LOVES GIULIA. There were rows of hearts drawn on the border wall of the lookout along with the occasional smiley face. A nearby bench read: SARA MI AMORE in two-foot tall letters.

The closer I looked, the more layers of graffiti I saw. Some faded messages had been left alone; others had been painted over with a more recent set of lovers. CEASERE + TIZI had overtaken GIORGIO + PINA. I kept expecting to find lewd messages, or the obligatory penis drawing that always seemed to show up in the States, but there was nothing like that. This was a sacred place.

Other Jonah didn't seem to care about the messages. He just walked along the seawall, looking out over the water. Then I saw him pull something from his pocket. It was a cell phone, and he looked down at the screen and smiled. He typed something into it. Then he just waited. Ten minutes later, a woman showed up and greeted him with a kiss. Her hair was pulled up in a ponytail and she had a camera around her neck.

She looked nothing like me.

I suppose that was inevitable. Why would Other Jonah be with Other Me? Of course, he'd be with my opposite. Still, I felt a pang of disappointment as I watched them pull out a map and point to something in the upper right-hand corner. And when he held her hand and they left the platform, I felt no urge to follow them. I just waved a hello, or maybe a good-bye, and watched them disappear.

Then I was alone on the platform. The other tourists had left, too. Off to take their rest like the locals maybe. I looked again at all the painted proclamations. Then I reached into my bag and dug around, hoping I had what I needed. Down at the bottom, among the cracker crumbs and old lipstick, I clasped a small marker. And when I pulled it out and tested it on the palm of my hand, it bled a dark purple.

I bent down and began writing my name. The wind from the sea sent the excess mist entwining with the salty air, and it felt good against my face. Gradually I made the plus sign along with Jonah's name after it. But I didn't stop there. I added one more word to the message. It was one I had seen on many of the others. The word: *SEMPRE*. I remembered enough of my high school Spanish to take a guess at the meaning. Like *siempre*, I thought, it must mean "always."

My walk back to the beautiful piazza was slow. I wandered the backstreets. I passed a small church called Chiesa

San Leonardo. It sat behind a small rectangular piazza that had been paved in a striking diamond pattern, and the top of the building pinched slightly at the top like a pope's hat. I kept going until I reached the Piazza Archimede. There was a fountain there made up of men riding sea creatures surrounding Diana, goddess of the hunt. The water cascaded in thin streams around her.

"I'm sorry," said a voice from behind me.

I didn't turn around. I just looked more closely at the fountain. There was some kind of a nymph escaping the outstretched arms of a man behind her. Diana stood between them, protecting the young woman.

"Listen. I didn't mean all of that about your dad. I guess all of this is catching up to me. We're actually here and I just want to do something great."

I admired Diana's bow and the stoic, badass expression on her face. Finally, I turned around and looked at Daniel. He was pink from the sun, and his eyes looked red. It was possible he'd been crying.

"Let's find a hotel," I said.

He nodded. I reached out my hand and he took it.

We walked back toward the temple and found a place nearby. We slipped inside a lobby, which had the same style columns as the temple. I let Daniel make the arrangements.

And when he got the room key, we walked up the stairs to our room and closed the door.

Then I pulled Daniel's shirt over his head and brought him close to me. He seemed tentative at first, but eventually he got the idea. He took off my tank top and unhooked my bra. And then we kissed and dropped onto the cool bed beside us. It was a nice kiss, a little hesitant, but his lips were warm and I felt the urgency building when I rolled on top of him.

"We can call this off," he said. "We can just go home if that's what you want."

"Do you have a condom?" I asked.

He held still.

"Yeah," he said in a sheepish voice.

He took his wallet out and removed one. It looked new.

"Are you sure you want to do this?" he asked.

"Yes," I said.

I unbuckled his belt and I unzipped my pants, and while I wish I could say we proceeded to have the most mind-blowing sex ever, that wasn't really the case. But we got over the initial awkwardness and it felt good after a while. I held tight to him and watched his shoulders tense. His face relaxed. And when we lay cooling on the bed afterward, an Italian game show played on the TV.

"Is this what being an adult is like?" I asked.

"Which part?" he said.

"Fighting and having sex and having no idea what you're doing?"

"I don't think adults have sex," said Daniel.

"Tell that to my dad," I said.

On the TV there was an older couple playing some kind of newlywed game. The man's face was turning bright red.

"Speaking of your dad . . ." said Daniel.

I looked away from the TV.

"What?"

"He's kind of been leaving me a lot of voice mails."

"Oh yeah?" I said. "Restaurant recommendations?"

Daniel didn't smile.

"The last one came an hour ago. He said he doesn't have a passport, but he's sending someone here to bring us home."

36

I woke up hours later in the dark of the hotel room, sweaty and unsure of where I was. I stumbled into the bathroom on wobbly legs and sat down on what I thought was the toilet. I didn't realize it was the bidet until I leaned back on the faucet and sent a powerful jet of ice-cold water straight up my back. I leaped up and smacked my hip on the sink. My hand searched out the light switch near the mirror, and finally the fluorescent bathroom flashed around me.

The bidet was still going off like a geyser behind me. I was shaking and dizzy and I wanted very badly to laugh, but I couldn't. So I just stood there for a moment, wholly aware of how confused and vulnerable I felt. I was in a bathroom in Sicily. I had just had sex with my dead boy-friend's roommate. And I had no idea what I was going to do next.

I turned off the cascading bidet and walked into the hotel bedroom. Daniel was still sleeping. He stirred a little beneath the rumpled sheets and then fell back asleep. I didn't regret what we had done. But I didn't quite know how to feel about it. I grabbed my phone and saw that there was a new message that wasn't from my father. I didn't recognize the number, but I knew who it was right away. It read:

I'm here, Tess.
Where are you staying?

I immediately wrote:

Meet me at the Ponte
Umbertino.

Then I pulled some fresh clothes from my bag and got dressed. I grabbed my room key and took the elevator down to the lobby where there was no desk clerk on duty. I continued out the door and into the streets of late night Siracusa.

The town was ghostly and I wondered if walking through it was the best thing to be doing right now. But once I got used to the quiet, and the feel of the stones beneath my feet, I felt my heart rate begin to drop.

I walked past the Chiesa San Leonardo, the lonely church that I had passed earlier. At night, it looked even smaller: just one door and a window, the entrance to its tiny courtyard chained off. I wondered if there were people buried beneath it. A few priests of local renown. Maybe a saint.

When I reached the Ponte Umbertino, I spied some drunken tourists, tottering home in the amber lights. On the other side of the water was a small wine bar. An *enoteca* Daniel had called it. Outside of it, a boy of about ten played the accordion and waited patiently for the occasional tip.

I took out my phone and turned on the camera. I pointed it at the scene in front of me and watched the world pulse in and out of focus. I hadn't taken a single picture since I arrived in Sicily. Now I had the sudden urge to capture all of it at once.

I went to press the digital shutter, but I heard footsteps behind me. And when I turned, I found a woman walking toward me from the other side of the bridge, and I knew it was her.

Grace the Rower.

She had come by land this time.

I expected to get a lecture right off the bat. Some tough love, or just toughness without the love. What I found was a woman in no shape to lecture anyone. Her lids were heavy, and her hair was spilling out of a loose tie. When she got closer, I noticed she was carrying a bottle of wine.

"It's table wine," said Grace. "I know because I took it from a table."

She sat down and set the bottle next to her. She closed her eyes and leaned against the side of the bridge.

"Grace," I said. "Are you okay?"

She didn't say anything for a moment. She just took a few deep breaths. Then she opened her eyes and pointed off toward the distance.

"Do you see that church out there? That giant cement teardrop? It's supposed to be the site of a miracle. Did you know that? There was a statue of the Virgin that wept actual tears for three days in the 1950s. Now people go there to see the origin of the miracle and pray for more."

I looked out over the city and found the church. I couldn't believe I hadn't noticed it before. It was the oddest-looking building I had ever seen. A gray conical structure coming to a point at the top.

"It looks like an upside-down ice-cream cone," I said.

Grace smiled, but only for an instant.

"Hey," I said. "Seriously. What's going on?"

"I'm here to bring you home," she said, and took a drink of wine.

I grabbed the bottle out of her hand.

"I understand that," I said. "But why are you drunk?"

She closed her eyes.

"Today's the anniversary," she said.

"Of what?" I asked.

"Of my daughter's death."

"Oh."

"It's been three years."

"Jesus," I said. "Why did you even come here? I'm fine. You must have known that."

She reached for the wine bottle. I held it away.

"Your father was so worried," she said. "He was a mess. And I thought it might help me to get away."

She paused.

"Also . . . I think I'm falling in love with your father."

I was too stunned by her remark to guard the bottle, and she quickly snatched it back.

"I hope that doesn't make you too uncomfortable," she said. "It probably does. But I was going to have to tell you sometime, so why not now in another country?"

I just stood there like an idiot. Grace started talking again.

"If someone had told me there was a place giving out miracles in Sicily or anywhere else when Avery got sick, I would have come. I would have done anything. Collected tears from a weeping statue. Even after she died, I would have been here."

An older couple spilled out of the *enoteca* and walked across the bridge, holding each other up for support. I watched them pass.

"This was where Jonah wanted to go," I said. "Part of me thought I might even find him here. I thought I saw him in the piazza, but there wasn't that spark."

Grace set her wine bottle on the ground. I picked it up and took a drink. It was sweet.

"I was in Italy after college," she said. "Somehow I forgot that everything around here is death-related. I was reading the guidebook on the plane. Just northwest of here is this place with five thousand tombs cut directly into the limestone. It's a huge seaside of cave graves. When your dad asked me to come here, I thought I might get away from death for a while. But I'm surrounded."

I sat down beside her. The bridge was empty now.

"Why do you love him?" I asked.

Grace looked at me.

"My dad," I mumbled.

"God. I don't know," she said. "He tries so hard."

"That's what you say about a puppy," I said.

"I admire it," she said. "He's really going for it. This wild idea of his. He believes."

She laughed.

"And he loves you, Tess. Getting to know you again, even like this. I think it's been the best thing for him. You should have seen his face when he found out where you were. He was minutes away from chartering a private plane."

I could hear the river lapping against the side of the bridge. I wondered if Jonah had seen this exact place where I was sitting on TV. If this was one of the places he imagined himself walking.

"Where is he, by the way?" asked Grace.

For a moment, I didn't know who she meant. Then it came to me.

"Back at the hotel, sleeping. I don't think he knows I'm gone."

"Does he know that you're still in love with his friend?"

The wine had left a sour aftertaste in my mouth. I tried to ignore it.

"I think so," I said.

She nodded and took a drink.

"How do you know when you're over someone. Someone who's gone?" I asked.

I took another drink of wine just to get the aftertaste out of my mouth.

"I don't know," said Grace. "I'll let you know if it ever happens."

Grace sat up straight against the bridge. Then suddenly she stood.

"Tess," she said, "if you just want to go home without doing anything here, that's fine. Just because you came here doesn't mean you have to go through with something if you're not feeling up to it anymore. It was brave enough just to do this."

She looked me in the eye.

"But if you want my help, I'm happy to work with you. Your dad told me you weren't too excited about us being together. That it felt like a betrayal. But you were my concern from the beginning. Ever since that day at the lake. And if there's anything I can do to help you through this, I want you to let me know."

She stood up and swayed in place. For a second, I thought she was going to tip over the rail and fall into the water below. I reached out and steadied her with a hand. Grace tried to take another pull from the wine bottle, but I held her arm.

"I need you to stop drinking," I said.

"And why would I do that?" she said.

"So you can tell me more about those caves by the ocean."

37

Daniel was awake when I found him in the hotel room. He was sitting on the double bed in a gray T-shirt and boxers. The curtains were pulled shut and the television was playing an Italian soap opera with no sound. His small duffel bag was packed and sitting on the luggage stand.

I stepped into the room, unsure of his mood, and sat down on the bed. The light of morning was just starting to peek around the curtains and Daniel's face was softened by it. Still, his dark eyes were fastened on me.

"It's all over," he said. "Isn't it?"

He licked his dry lips.

"No," I said. "It's not. Grace is here. We have an idea."

Daniel said nothing for a moment. He shifted in the bed, smoothing down the sleeves of his T-shirt.

"I meant us," he said.

He spoke the words quietly, just loud enough for me to hear.

"I don't know," I said. "I honestly can't answer that right now. There's a new plan, and we have to see it through."

His hands would not stop smoothing down his sleeves. When I touched his arm, he flinched.

"I thought you were gone," he said.

I opened my mouth to speak, but Daniel started again.

"I thought you went back to the States and left me here. I dragged us to this place, and I thought maybe you resented that. I had it all figured out. I was sure that's what happened."

"But it didn't," I said. "I'm here."

"You're here," he said.

I looked him in the eyes.

"I don't resent you. I had sex with you. Remember?"

"Yes."

"I don't have sex with people I resent."

He blinked.

"In fact," I said, "I don't really have sex with people. You should consider yourself lucky."

His eyes moved to the TV. There was a couple fighting. A handsome man with jet-black hair threw a lamp across the room.

"I'll tell you before I disappear," I said. "Okay?"

I touched his leg.

"Or I'll send you a message on Post-Life."

He smiled slightly.

"Do you have any real pants?" I asked.

"I'm sorry?" he said.

"Real pants," I said. "You know. Pants pants?"

"I think so . . ." he said.

"Great," I said. "I need you to put them on."

"Why?"

"Because we're going to a funeral."

The ride out of the city was hot and windy.

Grace rented us a van, and the air conditioner was broken. She drove into the morning sun with bloodshot eyes. I sat shotgun. And in the back, a quiet Daniel watched the rocky Sicilian landscape whip past the windows as the van headed out of Siracusa.

Behind us in a Fiat was Paul from the film crew. His other project had fallen apart, and his partner had gone home. But he was still here and game for our plan. Everything in the last few hours had happened so quickly that I was grateful for a moment to catch my breath. It was a thirty-minute drive to the Necropolis of Pantalica, home of the cave graves, and I hoped to use each one of those minutes to figure out what to do when we got there.

The desire to go to the caves had come to me so sharply on the bridge. And when it arrived, it was like a giant fist had finally unclenched in my chest. The city of Siracusa was the place for Other Jonah to live, not a place to put the real Jonah to rest. It would be better to put him in his own city of the dead like in that village cemetery I'd seen off the road.

"North of here," I read to Daniel from Grace's guidebook, "in Sortino, there is a limestone ravine. It was carved over thousands of years by two rivers. The Anapo and the Calcinara. Inside the ravine is a lush valley. Cut into the limestone cliffs of the gorge are over five thousand tombs as old as thirteenth century BC."

We wound around the blind curves of southeastern Sicily. We were over halfway to the magical tomb gorge, and I was finally becoming fully aware of what was happening around me.

"I probably should have mentioned this sooner," said Grace. "But I have no license to do any of this here. And I'm not exactly sure about the legality. This is a UNESCO World Heritage site."

She was driving erratically, nudging over the median on sharp turns, following the brown tourist signs for Pantalica. The windows were all open, and warm air was blowing through. Daniel didn't comment. The only thing he asked me when I told him what we were doing was about the cameraman.

"He's for Marian," I said. "To make a tape for Marian to see."

I didn't know that was his purpose until Daniel asked me, but then it was clear as day. I wanted her to be able to experience this, too, whatever it was going to be.

Eventually we made our way to the entrance of the trail, driving the last few miles on a smaller road, flanked by a rustic limestone wall, where each rock looked like a puzzle piece fit perfectly by an ancient mason. The sight was calming to me, brief evidence of a world where even the most jagged, random shapes could be pieced together into something whole.

When we arrived, the park wasn't open yet. But the barrier was easy to get over, and we all made the decision to trespass without talking about it. Grace seemed a little less hungover, but when I watched her almost topple over the small fence, it was hard to tell how much hiking she was going to be able to do.

"Your father would be appalled," she said, wiping beads of sweat from above her lips. "I was supposed to bring you back yesterday. And now look at me, breaking and entering. And I might still be drunk."

She took a long pull from a water bottle.

"My father has exploded dogs on a beach," I said. "He has no moral ground to stand on."

Daniel hopped the fence. And Paul swore under his breath, holding his camera over his head. Then the four of us stood together, the only inhabitants of the vast space. Our sole company were the birds, already well into their morning call-and-response. Grace finished her water, dabbing her temples with a few last drops.

"Do you have him with you?" she asked.

I nodded to Daniel and he pulled the container of Jonah's ashes from his pocket. The light caught the thin plastic lid and lit it up.

"Morning, Jonah," I said to the Tupperware.

I allowed for a small moment of silence. Then I walked to the path where the cement switched to dirt. Grace and Daniel followed. Paul carried his camera on a strap over his shoulder. It took us a few minutes to get within sight of the gorge, but when we came around that first corner and the valley unfolded before us, the four of us stopped without exchanging a word.

Beneath a scenic overlook was a landscape of sheer stone cliffs, carpeted by brush, and dotted with purple wildflowers and cacti. Carved into the sides of the canyon were thousands of identical square openings, black doorways and windows to the tombs. It was a high-rise of tomb-apartments inhabited by the souls of the ancient. And barely visible at the bottom was a glittering thread of ultramarine water.

"How far down do you want to go?" asked Daniel.

I didn't turn around.

"All the way," I said.

We began our descent, walking down the meandering path, past orchids and oleanders, and alongside the hollow cave tombs, which looked more like little Hobbit hovels than graves. Halfway down, I motioned to Paul and he began to film my downward climb. My internal chat started up, and I didn't resist it. I knew I had to speak to Jonah sometime.

Me: **Wild herbs and giant fennel along the path. A single falcon circling in the air. The sparkling river down to my left, growing closer with each step. The police officer on horseback fifteen feet below us.**

I blinked. When I looked down again, he was still there in his stylish baby blue uniform, on the back of a slow-moving horse.

"Oh shit," I whispered.

"What?" Daniel said, a little too loud.

I turned around and slapped a hand over his mouth. Then I pointed toward the edge of the cliff. Paul and Grace got the message and cocked their heads to listen. The sound of horse hooves clopping echoed up the trail.

I looked at Grace. She was dressed in one of her beige hippie funeral shrouds. Daniel held the container of ashes to his chest. Paul's camera equipment was much too large to hide. We did not look like we had accidentally shown up to the park in its off hours. We looked like we were up to some kind of illegal shit.

"Wait here," I whispered.

I left the manicured trail and tromped through the brush to the right, pushing low-hanging limbs from my path. There were thousands of tombs total, so I hoped it wouldn't take long to find one. I saw some soon enough, both high and low, but most were rectangular slots in the stone just big enough to shelve a single body. I went a few steps farther and came to an uneven stone ramp.

At the top was an entrance to a larger opening in the rock. I rushed back and found the others still waiting where I left them. The sound of the horse was getting closer. I waved them forward, and they began to jog, their legs whisking through wild grasses and over crunching sticks and jagged stones.

We reached the cave in a flurry, our shoes slipping on gravel, and ducked inside the dark interior, spooking the hell out of a family of roosting birds and a small lizard in the process. For the first five minutes, we waited in silence, too afraid to make a sound, listening for a cop on a pony to discover us and put us in an Italian jail.

From within the pitch black of the cavern, I could just see the horse trot past, the young policeman with sunglasses perched on his sunburned bald spot. He didn't look in our direction.

Still, the illusion of our isolation had been shattered. It was no longer early enough in the day to avoid the park's authorities. And there were bound to be more than one. There was no way around it: We were trapped in a cave for the time being.

At first, no one said anything. Paul was the first to move. He unsheathed a small flashlight from his pocket and switched it on. He shined it on us, making sure no one was injured. Grace's dress had certainly looked better an hour ago, but it was still in one piece. Daniel was exhausted but unharmed. And when the light shone on me, I found only a few scratches on my arms. So I stood up and began to feel along the walls of the chamber to see how far it went.

"Give me some light," I said, and Paul aimed his beam

toward me. I stepped deeper into the cave, hoping there were no bears in Sicily, or if there were, that they were very small, cute bears, and not the face-devouring variety.

Eventually, I began to feel some large bumps bulging out from the wall, and when the light caught up, it revealed them to be columns. They weren't structural, but purely ornamental. When I reached the very back of the cavern, it had been carved into a semicircle, and, at eye level, there were the faintest remains of frescoes.

"I don't think this is a tomb," Grace said.

I looked back toward the entrance, where she and Daniel were silhouetted against the light.

"What is it?" asked Daniel in a weary voice.

"I think it might be a church."

38

I had no speech prepared.

For the last two days, I had been trying to think of something. But, alas, there was nothing. Maybe it was the distraction of being in another country. Maybe it was whatever was happening with Daniel. But now I was standing in a medieval cave church, where everyone felt a little afraid of what might happen next, and my time was running out.

I knew there was a limited span in which this ancient cavern would still feel like an amazing discovery. It was a church carved into a cliff by people from so long ago that it was nearly impossible to imagine their lives. But, as incredible as that was, if I waited too long, the cave could easily transform back into just another dark musty space filled with bird droppings and invisible lizards. And I couldn't allow that to happen. So I said:

"Guys, I think we should get started."

At the sound of those words, everyone in the cave stood completely still and silent, and the trill of birdsong filtered in, echoing in the darkness. Then Grace nodded. Daniel held the bowl of ashes, and Paul adjusted his camera to the low light levels.

Meanwhile, I thought back to the one evening I'd spent with Jonah. The one at the farmhouse. It wasn't incredibly epic or romantic. And it wasn't the beginning of a love that anyone would much care about. But lying on the couch with him that night, I had felt the beginning of something, and it was indistinguishable from the reverberation of the music outside and the moonlight slanting in through the windows. And even though it had all eventually fallen apart, I still had that day and the way it felt. I had lived it, and it was mine forever.

I wanted to create one more day like that.

One more day worth keeping.

That was what I needed to do somehow in this hollowed-out chamber in Sicily. It was cool inside, but I was still sweating. I cleared my throat and stepped into the light of the doorway. I looked at Grace and at Daniel. And all I could think to say when I opened my mouth was something that had been replaying in my mind for months.

"This," I said, "was not how it was supposed to be."

The short sentence bounced around the cave, coming back to me word for word.

"I just want to be honest," I said. "It seems silly to do anything else at this point. The truth is that we're not supposed to be here, and we all know that. We're not supposed to be inside of a church made by old-timey people. We weren't supposed to bring Jonah here. We weren't supposed to hide from an Italian park ranger on horseback."

I paused and waited for my echoing voice to quiet.

"Also, maybe this is obvious, but Jonah was not supposed to die. Not yet. None of it was supposed to happen like this."

Grace eyed me quizzically.

"I don't mean to be bleak," I continued. "I know it sounds that way. What I mean is that nothing ever happens the way it's supposed to. Everything is messed up. Everything is flawed. And if we didn't have imperfection, I'm not sure what we would have left."

I looked out into the light outside. Its brightness compared to the darkness of the cave washed out what I could see of the landscape. Paul crouched down on one knee and pointed the camera up at me.

"The way I see it, we have a bunch of imperfect moments all lined up, one after the next, and we feel this strange, imperfect love. Then, before we know it, it's all over. We give everything we have, but that can never be enough to make things just the way we want them, or to keep someone with us as long as we'd like. But the struggle is worth something. And the love is worth something even though it's imperfect. And maybe we should try to celebrate this brief, incomplete thing we've been given. Maybe that's all we can do when we find ourselves in the dark."

Everyone remained quiet. I couldn't tell by looking at them how they felt about what I was saying. Still, no one interrupted me, so I kept going.

"Just because something didn't last as long as you needed doesn't mean it wasn't genuine. Jonah and I had an imperfect love. So what? That doesn't cancel it. And it's not gone. It's still here. And, today, I just want to bring it back. I want to make it tangible again for a little while."

I reached out for the ashes and Daniel handed the container to me. I opened the lid and stuck my hand inside. They were powdery and warm from Daniel's pocket.

"Jonah," I said. "This is Tess."

My voice was getting a little shaky, but I steadied it.

"Daniel is here, too. And I guess we came all the way here to say good-bye to you. If it's true that we knew you the best, I wish you had let us understand the whole of you. And I wish you'd felt more peace with who you were. But we can't change that. We can only celebrate what we knew. And, personally, I'm still glad I knew you."

I looked at Daniel. He nodded.

"And Daniel is too," I said.

I pulled out a handful of ashes.

"We're not erasing you," I said. "And we're not leaving you behind. But we need to put you somewhere. So you aren't . . . everywhere. I hope you get that."

I let go of the ashes and they drifted down to the floor of the cave church, passing through the light like smoke. I was about to reach my hand back inside, but then I stopped and handed the container to Daniel. His eyes were squinting in the light of the cave. I could tell he was struggling with what to say, but finally, he opened his mouth.

"I forgive you," he said, reaching his hand into the Tupperware. "And I forgive myself."

He let go of his handful, and the powder sifted through the air. Then Grace took the remainder of the container and stood over the spot I'd chosen.

"Earth to earth," she said. "Ashes to ashes. Dust to dust."

And while Paul kept his camera trained on us, she let the rest of them go. A breeze found its way inside, whistling through the cave. Some of the ashes swirled a bit in the air, but eventually, each grain, each tiny piece of Jonah settled on the ground between us. And then all I could do was walk out of the cave and slowly find my way back to the path.

Everyone else followed, tentatively at first. The trail was

steeper here and I removed my shoes to get a better grip. Paul stayed by the cave, pointing his camera over the edge of the trail to catch the rest of us shrinking into the gorge.

When I finally got down to the bottom, I walked, without speaking, alongside the river, which eventually dwindled into a rocky stream, and then finally to a bright, calm turquoise pool. I stood by it a moment, my face aimed toward the water.

Me: **The rocks in the pool, blurring in and out of focus. Small weeds billowing.**

I realized I was holding my breath. My heart was hammering in my chest, and I felt light-headed. But this time I was not alone, the way I had been on the dock in Minneapolis. I looked at Grace and Daniel.

Me: **The sunlight on the surface of the pool. The cool rocks on my bare feet.**

I waded in and felt the frigid water instantly numbing my feet and calves. The rocks on the bottom were smooth, and a little slippery from algae, but the water was perfectly clear. I could see my own feet walking as if I were seeing them through glass. I walked until the water deepened.

And inside my head, finally, there was no monologue to Jonah. Just the passing of my own thoughts. Including one that said: "Do you really want to do this?" And another that said: "Yes. It's okay."

So I stretched out my arms and plunged into the blue-green pool, yelling out from the cold, a muffled howl that barely made a noise underwater. I pushed myself forward with long strokes. And when I came to the surface, taking huge lungfuls of air, I felt the sun warm on my chilled skin.

Then Grace was floating next to me. She must have gotten in while I was under. Her dress gathered on the surface of the water, and on her face was something like contentment. Daniel jumped in last, and when he came up wet strands of hair stuck to his forehead, and he was shouting like a maniac. There might have been tears in his eyes. It was too wet to tell.

I swam over to him and held his hand under the cold water. Then we just floated. I don't know how long. My body was numb after a while, but that was okay. I didn't need it for the moment. The water held me up and drowned out all sound. I could have bobbed there the rest of the afternoon. But I knew it was risky to stay too long.

So instead, I tried to fully experience the moment and tell it to myself like a story. I had walked down a valley of jagged cliffs with black windows into ancient graves. I had rested on the surface of a pristine sky-blue pool. And for a minute or two, I found a place to be still. The light glittered on the water and it looked like the sun was beneath us, not above. Somehow I had found a little bit of life in a place of the dead.

39

By evening I was on a plane again.

The contrast was jarring. One moment I was outside my body, the next I was in a cramped cabin full of tourists. They were coming home from Italian vacations where they'd taken pictures in front of old things, eaten at overpriced restaurants, and spent most of the time on their phones. I could have been one of them.

Nobody knew I had just staged a funeral in a sea cave. Nobody knew that I was a high school dropout, my emergency credit card maxed. Nobody knew that I had absolutely zero clues about what I was going to do when I made it back stateside. And, most importantly, nobody knew that I had to say good-bye to the sleeping boy next to me when this plane touched down.

Daniel was in a Dramamine coma again. Or at least he appeared to be. His head was slumped down, chin on chest, and a single spot of drool dotting his thick lower lip. On the ride to the airport, we'd both sat shivering under a ratty blanket we found in the back of the van, too dazed to say much to each other.

We would be together on our first flight, but then we had to part ways. Daniel's parents hadn't been too thrilled to learn that their son was suddenly in another country. They were threatening to cut off their share of next year's tuition if he didn't come home right away.

All this came as a surprise to me. Somehow, I had assumed that Daniel would be coming back with me to stay at my dad's again when our voyage was over. But even as I articulated this thought to myself, I could see it was ridiculous. My father had threatened his life. It was probably safe to say that his couch privileges had been revoked. So we had the length of an international flight to say good-bye.

Only we didn't seem to be doing that.

Instead we were watching bad movies. One after the next, pressing play at the same time on the touchscreens attached to the seats in front of us, and staring forward like lobotomy patients. We were swilling ginger ales and eating bags of "lightly salted" peanuts. We didn't laugh. We didn't cry. We stared.

Then the movies were over and I was left watching

Daniel drool. Grace was somewhere at the back of the plane. When we'd found out there were seats together this time, she'd wordlessly given them to Daniel and me. Maybe if she'd been closer, she could have cut the tension.

"I've been thinking . . ." he said suddenly. ". . . about when I go back to school."

I had been zoning out. When my vision refocused, I saw he had one eye open.

"Jesus. Don't do that," I said.

"Do what?"

"Just start talking out of a deep sleep. It's freaky."

He opened his other eye.

"I haven't been sleeping," he said. "I've been thinking."

"You could have fooled me."

"And we have to talk about this."

I took a deep breath. I took my earbuds out and he calmly started to talk.

"I've been pushing this around in my mind, and I keep coming back to two basic options. And, to be perfectly honest, they both seem a little crazy to me. The first one is that we say good-bye at the airport and that's it. We said our farewell to Jonah, so our reason for . . . being together is gone if you think about it in one way."

I watched his face. It betrayed nothing.

"And the second option is that I go back home, and in a couple months, back to school, and then . . ."

"Don't say it," I said.

"I have to say it at least once."

"No you don't."

He sighed.

"Long distance," he said.

"E-mails?" I said.

"Among other things. I mean, you have to admit, it's how we started."

"It's how *you* started," I said.

This stung; I could tell. But he didn't break eye contact.

"I don't think I can do it," I said.

He rested his hands on his tray table. His fingernails were chewed to nothing.

"What if there were rules?" he said.

"Like what?"

"I don't know," he said. "Things to make it more . . ."

He paused for longer than he needed.

"Real," I said.

"Yes. That."

He slumped lower in his seat and looked at the screen in front of him.

"What if we can only send one message a day, and the

rest is by phone or video chat, so that there's something more to it. And . . ."

"I can't do it," I said.

"Tess."

"I'm sorry," I said. "I'm not trying to be unreasonable. I just can't do it. It sounds like hell to me. Returning to hell."

This quieted him. I hadn't meant for it to come out so harsh, but there it was. I'd said it. I watched Daniel's face fall. I took a sip of ginger ale and the bubbles stung my nostrils.

We both sat there for a moment, until the roar of the engines was the only thing I could hear. Then, eventually, Daniel turned away and I put my earbuds back in, and we sat in excruciating silence for the next hour or so as the plane made its way back to American airspace.

We landed at O'Hare. We trudged through customs. And we walked through the cheesy neon light thing on the moving walkway that I loved when I was a kid. Grace kept her distance—probably as much for her well-being as ours. We were almost to the crossroads of our gates when Daniel finally stopped and just stood there, holding his duffel bag in the fluorescent light of the airport.

He looked completely drained. I'm sure I did, too.

Someday I would have to ask myself why the guys I liked were always so sad. But that was a question for another time. I walked up close to him.

"It's been nice getting to know you, Daniel Torres," I said. Then I paused. "Actually, it's been kind of fucked up and strange. But nice too. Not without its nice moments. Anyway . . . thank you."

"For what?" he said.

He seemed genuinely shocked to hear my words.

"For making all the stupid decisions that made this possible."

He just looked at me.

"I mean it," I said. "Without them, I'm not sure where I'd be."

His face turned a little red, and I couldn't tell if he was going to laugh or cry or maybe just tell me to go to hell. Instead he said:

"I just don't know yet, Tess."

"Know what?"

He took a step to the side and looked down.

"Who we are without him."

I met his eyes. There was sleep in the corner of one. I had the sudden urge to wipe it away.

"Me neither," I said.

Around us people were dragging their suitcases past us, going around the two-person obstacle in their path without a second thought. Ours was a movie that played occasionally at airports. Everyone had seen it before.

"We could find out," I said.

He nodded.

"Yeah," he said. "We could."

But he didn't sound convinced.

"Letters," I said.

"What?" said Daniel.

I wasn't sure I had really said the word until it came out again.

"Letters," I repeated. "I would like you to write me letters."

His lips parted. I kept talking.

"I want you to use a pen and write things to me on a piece of paper," I said. "It doesn't matter what kind. And then put that paper in an envelope and put a stamp on that envelope. And send it to me. And I'll do the same thing. For you."

His eyes narrowed.

"I haven't written a letter since I was a kid," he said.

"Great," I said. "So you know how."

He looked at his phone. He needed to get to his gate. His next flight would be boarding soon.

"What if they're terrible?" he said. "What if they're so terrible, I can't send them?"

I closed my eyes.

"Then you can't," I said.

We looked at each other one more time. This was the part in the movie where we were supposed to fall into each other's arms. But I guess we didn't get the script because he just turned and walked off toward his gate.

I watched him join in with the other travelers. Some were walking like the undead. Others were seated at gates nearby, tapping screens, watching real movies, reading books. They were staring wide-eyed at the stories they'd chosen, looking for a way to pass the time, until they arrived at their final destination.

40

The morning after I returned from Sicily, I woke before dawn in my father's empty house thinking about my own funeral. The death of the universe was too big. It would have to wait. Instead, I'd made a new promise to myself to keep my worries in the realm of things I could control. Thus: my funeral. There were so many options, though. That's what had me thinking in the predawn hours. And my current ideas were too varied to be of any real help.

I could be incinerated into dust, for example.

Or made into nutrients in the soil.

I could be fireworks in the night sky.

Or particles in a memorial reef on the ocean floor.

There was even a company pressing people's ashes into vinyl records, so someone could play a Beatles record made out of me, and sing along to my tiny bits. I could be embalmed and placed on a motorcycle like a man in Michigan. Or be posed in a boxing ring like a guy in Mexico. I could be frozen. I could be shattered and planted beneath a tree. And this was all just the first step in the process. There was so much to consider.

I walked downstairs and found my father gone, I didn't know where. He had barely spoken to me since I got home. I'd been waiting for a reaction from him since I first dropped out of school, and now I finally got one. Stony silence. He didn't say much at the airport. Or at the baggage claim. It was only on the car ride on the way home, where he temporarily opened the floodgates.

"I don't want you to think I'm not angry about this, Tess," he said. "Because I am. I really am."

"Really?" I said. "I could hardly tell by your brooding."

He gave me a look that told me sarcasm wasn't going to be a good strategy here.

"But mostly I'm just hurt," he said.

I looked at his tired face. He hadn't shaved in a couple days and his jaw was shadowed with stubble. He'd told Grace he hadn't slept while I was gone.

"I thought we were fixing things," he said.

He blinked into the early morning sunlight.

"I thought you were actually going to tell me what was going on in your life. I wanted to be that person. I was ready. But I guess that's just not going to happen with us, is it?"

I was starting to prefer his silence.

"I know I've made mistakes," he said, "I get that. And I know you think I sabotaged our family. But it's not that simple, Tess. You don't know everything. You're old enough to understand some complexities."

"What do you mean?" I said.

"It's not worth talking about."

"Then how do I know you're not lying?"

He sighed.

"Look," he said. "There were certain indiscretions."

"Dad," I said. "Will you stop speaking in code? If you want to tell me something, tell me."

"Your mother was having an affair," he said.

I felt my mouth close tight.

"With that guy she's seeing now. And I wasn't entirely in denial, the way you think I was."

He opened the lid on a thermos, and the smell of his burnt coffee filled the car.

"It's easy to imagine that since I was so checked out, but the truth is I was in mourning. There's a difference. I knew my marriage was dead, and I couldn't help grieving for it. It swallowed up everything else, and I walked around in a fog. For years I guess."

"But you were trying out all those jobs . . ."

"A distraction," he said. "A way to get away from home."

"God, I can't believe her," I said.

He took a sip of coffee.

"It wasn't just her, Tess. You don't need to make her

your super villain. I wasn't the world's greatest husband."

I looked in the rearview mirror and watched the road disappear behind us.

"She didn't even come to get me," I said.

"What do you mean?" he asked.

"In Sicily. I thought maybe she'd show up to bring me home."

My dad was quiet a moment.

"That was never going to happen," he said.

"Why not?"

He took another loud sip of coffee.

"Because I never told her you were there."

"Oh," I said. I paused to let that sink in.

"How do you think it makes me look?" he said. "The one time you're with me in the last two years and you flee the country. I knew there was some tension between us, but I didn't think it was this bad."

"It was for a funeral," I mumbled.

"I know," he said. "That makes it even worse! Funerals are what I do!"

"Dad . . ." I said.

"I don't want to hear anything else now. I just want to let you know I've made a decision. And I'm afraid it's a final one."

"What decision?"

"I don't think we should work together anymore," he said.

He said it low and quiet, like it was hard to get out.

"It was an irresponsible idea to begin with, and it has now run its course."

I expected to feel nothing after he said this. After all, I had been helping *him*. I was doing the favor. But there was a pit in my stomach after he spoke, and I felt it all the way home. I felt it when I went to bed that night. And I still felt it when I woke up thinking of my funeral.

When my dad finally came home, I found him making business calls at the kitchen table. After he got off the phone, I asked him if there was a new funeral he was planning, but he didn't answer me.

"C'mon," I said. "What is it? A funeral for a stray cat? A marmoset?"

Silence.

"Just give me a hint."

More silence.

Eventually I went upstairs and called Grace. I asked her if I could come over for a little while. Surprisingly enough, she told me to pack a bag and stay for the weekend.

"Your dad just needs more time to get over it," she said.

"Over what exactly?" I asked.

"His heartbreak."

"Oh," I said.

41

So I showed up with a backpack and sat on Grace's balcony while she went to work. There was an egg-shaped wicker chair hanging outside of her small, stylish apartment downtown and I claimed it for my own.

It had been a while since I lived with a woman and the perks were pretty awesome right off the bat. Cleanliness, for one. Grace did a natural deep clean of her entire apartment every weekend, she told me. And she used a fancy cider vinegar that made the whole place smell like apples. Also, there were no freakishly long pubic hairs on the toilet seat, so that was a plus.

Another perk was the grocery shopping. Grace's fridge was stocked with organic produce, and I was given full access. I began to eat fruits and vegetables like a sailor staving off scurvy. And finally, there was the library, mostly composed of books about the alternative death movement. After spending some time just scanning the shelf, I began to read through them, taking in large gulps of information about backyard burials and nature cemeteries.

That evening, Grace still wasn't home, so I ignored my best instincts and went into her home office. I only had to look in two drawers before I came across the baby pictures. Grace appeared in one after the other, along with a man with the same blue eyes and turned-up nose as the child. And, of course, the closer I looked, the more the baby girl resembled Grace, too. Her hair was an identical shade for one thing. And her top lip curved in just the same way.

Later that night, over vegan lasagna and a glass of wine, I asked her if I could volunteer at Greener Pastures the next day. Grace looked surprised, but only for a few seconds. She finished chewing a bite of lasagna, and simply said, "I don't know how your dad will feel about that."

But I showed up the next morning and she didn't turn me away. So, for the next week, while I waited for my dad to talk to me again, I went to Grace's office in Northeast Minneapolis. Mostly, I helped with record keeping and answering the occasional phone call while Grace's assistant was at lunch. But a few days in, I began to keep a blog, writing short entries about hand-carved stoneware urns, funeral photographers, recycling pacemakers, and finally, on day five, I began an extensive entry about how to remove deceased family members from social media.

I started it with no trouble, writing about proof of authority and login information. It was only when I felt the urge to comment on the topic that I froze up. By the end of the morning, I broke down and visited Jonah's Facebook page. The page had not been taken down like I thought. Instead, in the time since I'd last checked it, it had become a full-on memorial page.

"Missing you, J!" wrote a former classmate. "Had a dream last night that you were still here, man. Wish it were true." "Your birthday's coming up, soon. I didn't forget!" Extended family were present, too: "We'll be setting a place for you at the lake this year, Jonah. Be sure to pay us a visit." "Hope you're enjoying your journey." "Your cousin just graduated high school. I know you'd be proud!" I scrolled down the page.

Since I wasn't a "friend" anymore, I didn't have access to all the pictures, but I was surprised to find that I still had most of them memorized. There were so many times I'd used them as placeholders to picture him when I hadn't seen his face in months. I wasn't sure how long I'd been staring at the screen when Grace tapped me on the shoulder. I jumped.

"Sorry," she said. "I didn't mean to scare you."

I didn't answer, and Grace looked at the screen over my shoulder.

"There's a food truck down the street with decent tacos. You ready for lunch?"

It would have been so easy to say no, to say I was almost finished with my blog post. But I darkened the computer screen in front of me and stood up. I followed Grace out the door and out onto the street. Summer was here in earnest and I was sweating the instant the hot sun hit my neck.

"You've been doing some nice work on the blog," Grace said. "I've gotten a lot of compliments."

"Thanks," I said. "I'm glad."

"I think it's time to start paying you for it."

I heard myself laugh.

"I'm eating all of your food," I said. "I live in your house."

"That can't be a permanent arrangement, Tess. You understand, right?"

The information didn't entirely register with me. I didn't want to hear it.

"But I'd like you to keep the blog going," she said. "I think it will be a good part-time job when you go back to school."

I slowed my step.

"I dropped out of school," I said.

"You dropped out of *a* school," said Grace. "One school. For reasons of bereavement and mental distress. I think we can find you another one."

We were approaching the taco truck.

"Listen, Tess," said Grace, "I think you have a hell of a lot to offer this industry if that's what you want to do with your life. You are a smart, capable, deeply empathetic person, and those are the skills you need to actually do this. But I also think you're a seventeen-year-old in the final stages of mourning, and you don't need to do something forever because it helped you through a difficult time."

I shielded my eyes against the sun.

"There are plenty of other ways to contribute. And you need time to figure that out. Finish high school. Go to college. Find out what you want. Find out what you don't want. Screw up some more. Get your heart broken again. Try to be decent along the way. That's how you make a life."

Grace got in the line behind one other person.

"It's easy to get stuck. To let one big thing hold you in place. And it's such a waste. Don't fall for it. It will keep you from everything."

Grace paused for a breath. I looked over at her.

"That can't be all your advice," I said.

She smiled.

"No!" she said. "It's not. Get the HPV vaccine. And order some tacos, for Christ's sake! I'm starving."

I ordered and when my tacos came out, I took a small bite of the first one. It tasted good. So salty it stunned my tongue. The two of us ate and watched the crowd build at the taco truck. A couple of pierced boys rode by on tall bikes, and I watched them pedal away with purpose. Eventually, we finished and got up to walk back to the office. When I got back to my desk, she brought me something.

"Here," she said. "Your dad gave me this. It came to his house yesterday."

She held out a single letter, and I grabbed it with my thumb and forefinger. I looked at it for a moment. His handwriting, in blue pen, was messy but legible. Eventually, I opened it up. It said:

Dear Tess,

I don't know how to write letters. That will become very apparent soon. I don't think I've written one since I went to 4-H camp the summer after fifth grade and got a tick on my eyelid. In fact, I'm so out of practice, I had to type this out first, and now I'm transferring it to my mom's stationery with a pen, which explains the flowers on the bottom of each page. I hope you like begonias.

Anyway, this isn't going to be a long letter. I know much has already been said. And I don't want to rehash our conversation from the airport. In fact, I'd like to forget that airport ever happened, maybe. Instead: I just want to do something small. I don't know why, but I want to tell you about the first time I met you.

It was November, I think. And I had just come back from a night class to find my dorm room dim. There was a video game glowing on the TV, a little sword-wielding avatar running in place, frozen in his mission. I didn't see Jonah at first. He was on his bed, taking deep breaths and rubbing his temples. I asked him if he was okay, and he said yeah. Just a headache. No big deal. A week earlier I might have believed him. But he'd been having a lot of these "headaches" lately, and I was starting to suspect that maybe there was something more going on.

But I sat down at his desk nearby and asked him if he needed anything. He said yes. I was thinking Advil maybe. A glass of water. But when I asked him what, he said he needed me to respond to you.

Now I had heard all about you at this point. Jonah had told me about Iowa and the way you guys continued talking online. He told me that you were beautiful. That you were *funny. That he wished he lived in Iowa so he could be with you all the time. And I believed him, of course. He didn't lie about people.*

So you guys had been g-chatting, I guess, and apparently he had just walked away to lie down. But he forgot to tell you. He forgot to sign off. And that's what he wanted me to do.

"What should I say?" I asked him.

"Doesn't matter," he said. "Anything. Just say I have homework or something."

"As you, though."

"Right," he said.

So, that's what I did. I wrote in his voice, some excuse about having homework and that I needed to sign off. And I would have left it at that, but you wrote back really fast.

"You never gave me an answer . . ." you said.

I looked over at Jonah. He was wincing.

"To what?" I wrote.

"Jesus," you said. "You have short-term memory problems."

"I know," I wrote.

Then you wrote: "The million-dollar question: Would you rather have no penis or five?"

I laughed out loud at that point, I think. And I asked Jonah the question. But he didn't answer. He was asleep, or pretending to be. I glanced back at the screen and you had written again.

"Just kidding, Now quit stalling and tell me if you've ever been in love."

I watched the blinking cursor. And I thought about coming clean about my identity right then. But it didn't seem right to mess up this moment. That was one of my justifications. And given what I knew about Jonah, I felt like I could answer the question honestly. That was the other. So, I answered it. I wrote:

"Not until now."

You took a moment to write back. And then you wrote: "Sorry, but I'll never fall for a man with five penises."

And I said: "That's okay because I don't have one at all."

And then you sent a smile and signed off.

On the one hand, it felt like nothing much had just happened. I had flirted for a friend. And I had done a decent job, I guess. On the other hand, it started to occur to me that I had just told you Jonah loved you. In so many words. But I don't think I was writing for Jonah in that moment.

I know it's absurd. I had no right. I understood that on some level. You didn't know me. And really, I didn't know you. But I felt like I did. Or maybe, as I tried to explain before, I just wanted to be part of it.

And I knew already that Jonah was starting to retreat

from you. He was ducking away from everything, and I didn't know why. I just knew he was going to let you go, and I didn't want that to happen. So, at first, I thought what I was doing was selfless. I was keeping love alive.

However imperfect.

I know now that I was doing something else. And I wish everyday that I had met you under different circumstances. That you knew me as a different person. But I don't think we would have met in any other way, Tess. And I think now that maybe what I was doing was reaching out to someone else who knew this amazing person. Someone who might be able to help me as he slowly disappeared from my life.

I guess this turned into a long letter.

The only thing I want to say before I stop this thing is that I don't know what created this feeling for me. But I don't care. I would like you to be a part of my life. If I have to write more of these letters, I will. And if I have to come to Minnesota once a month to convince you to be my friend, I will. But, in the end, my answer was true that day.

I have only been in love once.

I was crying when Grace came back to my desk. She just stood there for a moment, unsure what to do. But eventually, she put a hand on my shoulder and then leaned in.

"It's slow," she said. "There are no clients. Why don't you go home for the day?"

I wiped my nose on the sleeve of my shirt.

"I'll just ride back with you when you're done," I said.

"No," she said. "I mean *home* home."

I was still holding the letter. Now I started to fold it back up.

"Oh," I said. "There."

She opened her purse and dug out some money. She handed me a twenty-dollar bill.

"I called you a cab," she said. "I can bring your stuff by later."

"Grace," I said, but I started to cry again.

"It's okay," she said. "I know."

42

I walked out onto the street where there was already a taxi waiting for me. And I hopped inside. As the guy took off toward my father's neighborhood, I came back to myself a little, and I remembered that I hadn't finished my blog entry. I had left it half-done on the computer. I knew it would be there for me when I came back. It wasn't a big deal. But I had this itch of unfinished business. Finally, it hit me that it wasn't the blog I was thinking about.

I pulled out my phone and broke every rule I had set up. I texted Daniel.

> **There's one last thing we need to do.**

I waited a few minutes and then his reply came back.

What's that?

I wrote back immediately.

Take him off-line. I know you
have the passwords. It's time.

There was a significant pause this time. So I wrote again.

All the accounts you wrote
me from. They shouldn't be there
anymore. They aren't ours.

I know. But it just seems
like the end of something.

It's not the end.
You said so yourself.

There was another pause then a new message.

You got the letter.

I did.

I realized something after I sent it.

What?

You never answered the question
yourself. On that first day.

That's true.

I waited. He sent no follow up. He was waiting for me.

> My answer has changed
> since then.

Still nothing from him. I wrote:

> I have been in love twice.

It came so easily from my fingertips that I immediately suspected it wasn't true. But when the tears came back, I knew that it probably was. He wrote:

You owe me a letter, Tess Fowler.

Then:

I'll leave the FB page for
a memorial. Everything else
will be gone by tonight.

> And then what happens?

Like you said:
Something imperfect.

And then before he signed off:

I'll be watching my mailbox.

I put the phone in my pocket and I looked out the cab window as the heat of the afternoon made waves in the air of the city. It was just before rush hour, and the roads were nearly empty. After the driver got off the freeway, we passed a public high school. A long brick building with what looked like hundreds of small windows. It was out for the summer, and an American flag flapped lazily in the light breeze. Is that where I'd end up going? It was unimaginable.

The cab pulled up at my father's house, and I gave him Grace's money and got out. Part of me expected to see her Jeep parked in the driveway with her rowing shell on top. But of course, she wouldn't have put me in a cab just to drive here herself.

I walked through the screen door and let it slap closed behind me. The house was a little cleaner than usual, and in the hallway, I noticed the tacky wallpaper had been stripped down. It sat in sheets along the wall.

"Dad!" I said.

There were buckets of paint by the staircase, and the first few steps were painted a clean white color instead of the dingy brown that used to be there. There was plastic on the railing.

"Dad," I said. "Are you having a nervous breakdown?"

No answer. I kept walking until I got to the living room where I found my father on the couch with tears in his eyes.

"You are having a nervous breakdown," I said.

He didn't look up at me. His eyes were fixated on the television. I followed his gaze and saw myself. I saw myself in a cave in Sicily. He was watching the footage. As far as I knew, we had not received it from Paul yet. But now it was playing in my dad's living room.

"Where did you get this?" I asked.

Again, he didn't look up. He pointed to an open envelope on the coffee table. I recognized the return address as Grace's.

He motioned for me to sit down. So, I walked across the room and sat on the ratty couch next to my father, who was covered in splatters of paint and a gummy substance that was probably wallpaper paste. He put his arm around me, and I didn't care that he was getting paint on me. Then I looked back at the screen. The dust was swirling in the air, glittering in the Mediterranean light. And all of us were standing silent.

"I liked what you said," he whispered.

I nodded.

"It wasn't bad," I said.

Paul was shooting us walking down the trail now. Moving toward the valley below. As the angle of the light changed, we looked like silhouettes against the rock face.

I looked away from the screen. The walls of the living

room were scraped down, too. Patches of old paint colors were coming through.

"Are you tearing this place down?" I asked.

He smiled.

"I thought I'd make it habitable now that there're two of us."

"Two of us?" I asked.

He nodded.

"Does that mean I'm getting a bedroom?"

"If you mean a room with a bed," he said. "Then yes. You are getting one of those. If you don't max out any credit cards this week, you might even get a dresser."

He chuckled at his own joke. And he was already walking out of the room into the kitchen where he had something going for dinner. I thought about following him in. I wanted to ask him more about my room. But instead, I sat there and watched the end of the footage.

We were so far down now that Paul couldn't get us in focus. If I squinted, I could see us moving. But it was hard to tell. He tried to zoom in, but we were indistinguishable from the water below. I know I was down there. But everything around me was so big and dazzling there was no way to find me.

And maybe, I thought, that was okay.

ACKNOWLEDGMENTS

Hello, reader. The book you have just finished almost never happened. I don't mean to be dramatic, but there was a time when I thought I would never figure out how to make it work. It took years to find its voice and without the help of some wonderful people, I'm not sure it would ever have made it there. So, here goes:

First of all, thank you to Junita Bognanni for reading a 470-page draft of this book four times. Four times! And for listening to me talk about funeral practices at the dinner table for three years. Also, thank you for marrying me. Have I said that enough? You will always be my first reader, and the one who matters most.

Thank you to Kathy Bognanni, who has read more books than anyone I know, and who gave me a no-nonsense reading along with a vision of what this book could be. Thank you to Cecil Castellucci for a revelatory conversation about Young Adult literature in a crowded bar in Minneapolis, and for an agent recommendation that changed everything. Thank you, Kirby Kim, agent of agents, for guiding this thing perfectly and giving me the encouragement to finish it. I'm happy to have you as a friend and a partner in crime. Thank you, too, to Brenna English-Loeb, Cecile Barendsma, and everyone else at Janklow & Nesbit.

An enormous thank you to Namrata Tripathi, my phenomenal editor. You understood this book better than I did when we first spoke on the phone, and you have challenged and supported me every step of the way. It has been an honor to work with you. And thanks to Lily Yengle, my amazing publicist, and everyone at Dial Books for Young Readers.

I first began this book at the American Academy in Rome on the best fellowship an artist can receive. Thank you to the Academy and to the readers who selected me for an experience where I met some of the greatest humans on the planet and sang in the hardest-working Sinatra cover band this side of the Janiculum Hill.

Thank you to my colleagues and students at Macalester College, who inspire me on a daily basis. Readers, givers of advice, and amateur mental health professionals include: Tarik Karam, Matt Burgess, Nick Dybek, Ethan Rutherford, Hamlett Dobbins, Peter Livolsi, and Alex Albright.

Thank you to my guru, and father, Sal Bognanni, and to Mark Bognanni, the smartest person I know. Thank you to all the Bognannis and all the Rhynas crew for your love and unwavering belief in me.

Finally, to Roman Bognanni: I was writing this book in the hospital after you were born, wondering, after I looked at your tiny face, how I would ever finish another novel again. Now I know: I just have to look at myself the way you look at me, and then sit down at the computer. I can't wait to hear the stories you invent.